M000307977

Praise for the Harrison Weaver Mysteries

Undertow of Vengeance, Joseph Terrell's fourth thriller in the Harrison Weaver crime writer series, and set in North Carolina's Outer Banks, is a knockout. With the deadpan savvy delivery of Humphrey Bogart as Sam Spade and the clipped declarative sentences of Dashiell Hammett, this volume, like its predecessors, reaches out in the very first sentence, grabs you by the lapels, and never lets up.
—Joseph Bathanti, North Carolina Poet Laureate

Smooth writing from an eloquent storyteller goes down like fine scotch. *Undertow of Vengeance* is a keeper.
—Maggie Toussaint, Author, Cleopatra Jones Mysteries

"Every once in a while I'll pick up a book and from the first sentence, I'm engaged. Written with an extraordinary eye for detail yet in the sparse language of the journalist he once was, Terrell's novel is filled with wonderful dialogue, believable characters and just enough plot twists to keep the reader turning pages."
—Kip Tabb, Editor, *North Beach Sun*

"Joe Terrell gets the Outer Banks just right, from crashing surf to the sordid crimes behind the tourism façade, to a thoughtful sleuth who can throw a punch and make a mean sweet tea."
—David Healey, Author, *The House That Went Down With The Ship*

"A smart, savvy combination of who-done-it and police procedural."
—Kathryn R. Wall, Author, the Bay Tanner Mysteries

Books by
Joseph L.S. Terrell

Harrison Weaver Mysteries

TIDE OF DARKNESS
OVERWASH OF EVIL
NOT OUR KIND OF KILLING
UNDERTOW OF VENGEANCE
DEAD RIGHT RETURNING

Jonathan Clayton Novels

THE OTHER SIDE OF SILENCE
LEARNING TO SLOW DANCE

Stand Alones

A TIME OF MUSIC, A TIME OF MAGIC

A NEUROTIC'S GUIDE TO SANE LIVING

DEAD RIGHT RETURNING

A HARRISON WEAVER MYSTERY

JOSEPH L.S. TERRELL

DEAD RIGHT RETURNING
ISBN 978-1-62268-079-5

Copyright © 2015 by Joseph L.S. Terrell

All rights reserved, including the right to reproduce this book or portions thereof in any form whatsoever. For more information contact Bella Rosa Books, P.O. Box 4251 CRS, Rock Hill, SC 29732. Or online at www.bellarosabooks.com

This book is a work of fiction. Names, characters, places and incidents are products of the author's imagination or are used fictitiously. Any resemblance to actual events or locales or persons, living or dead, is entirely coincidental.

First Printed: May 2015

Library of Congress Control Number: 2015940964

Also available as e-book: ISBN 978-1-62268-080-1

Printed in the United States of America on acid-free paper.

Cover photograph and design by Roo Harris and K. Wilkins.
Author photograph by Christopher Terrell.

Book design by Bella Rosa Books

BellaRosaBooks and logo are trademarks of Bella Rosa Books

10   9   8   7   6   5   4   3   2   1

This book, with my thanks and appreciation, is for Edward Greene of the Christmas Shop in Manteo, North Carolina.

Acknowledgments

I want to thank former State Bureau of Investigation agents Jeff Freeman, Fred McKinney, and Thomas Childrey for their willingness to talk with me about law enforcement of the drug trade. A special thanks to manuscript readers Gale Anne Friedel and Veronica Moschetti for their insightful edits and comments; they made the book better. In putting this story together, I was delighted to have the gracious cooperation of Edward Greene, owner of the Island Gallery and Christmas Shop. Last but certainly not least, I want to thank my editor and publisher Rod Hunter of Bella Rosa Books for his continuing support and faith in me as a writer.

—*JLST*

Author's Note:

Most of the places mentioned in this story exist on North Carolina's Outer Banks, and while several of the names in this book are those of real people, the villain, those associated with him, and the victims exist only in my imagination. They are real to me, but they are all made up. This is, after all, a work of fiction. That's what storytelling is all about. Once again I picture the historic Dare County courthouse in Manteo as it was employed years ago to house the sheriff's and other offices.

–JLST

As every boater knows, when returning to harbor, red channel markers should be on the starboard. Thus the mantra: Red Right Returning.

DEAD RIGHT
RETURNING

Chapter One

Tom Applewaite and his younger brother Willie Boy drove south toward Stumpy Point in their five-year old Nissan. They didn't talk much. At least Tom didn't. Willie Boy came up with sporadic chatter every few miles, commenting on the flat marshy landscape with stands of pines on both sides of Highway 264 out of Manteo. They passed a sign that cautioned black bears might be nearby, and Willie Boy said, "I wish we could see a black bear. I'd like to see one of them things." Tom nodded solemnly and concentrated on his driving.

Tom's thoughts were about negotiating with John Livermore to rent his boat for twenty-four hours. It had already been tentatively settled but Tom knew there was reluctance on Livermore's part. He would be paying Livermore twenty-five thousand dollars for the use of the boat. With his right hand, Tom touched the bulge of bills in the side pocket of his faded jeans, just to reassure himself. It was a lot of money that he had been entrusted with. He and Willie Boy could simply continue driving and keep the twenty-five thousand dollars. It would last them a good while. However, *they* wouldn't last as long as the money would. The people in charge would have them killed. He and Willie Boy wouldn't survive more than a few days.

Tom was excited and proud about being part of the operation, to be in charge of bargaining for the use of Livermore's boat for twenty-four hours, and to offer him the big wad of money, acting the big shot. He was pleased with himself.

John Livermore's house was on the left and was set back about fifty yards from the narrow paved road, the edges of which cracked and buckled each winter with freezing and with heavy downpours of rain. Although there hadn't been any hard freezes so far this unusually mild December, cold weather was bound to come, and more asphalt would be needed to patch the road. To avoid the crumbly edges, Tom drove mostly in the middle of the road. There was virtually no traffic, and he didn't even bother to engage his turn signal as he pulled into the sandy driveway that served John Livermore's house. The frame house itself appeared to have been built in stages, and with different materials, and with varying design thoughts in mind with each stage. The house backed up to the deepwater canal, and Livermore's twenty-five foot Ranger boat was tied to a sun-bleached wooden dock. The boat was glowing and pristine in the midmorning sun and didn't look like it could belong to the owner of the house, but it did.

Tom cut the ignition on the Nissan and he and Willie Boy stepped out of the car into the sunlight. Willie Boy stretched, looked around at their surroundings, and grinned. "Don't see any black bears," he chuckled.

Tom didn't say anything but kept his eyes on the front porch. John Livermore opened his wooden front door and then pushed the screen door and stood on the edge of the low porch. He wore a brown windbreaker not zipped, and a baseball cap pulled on tight. The sun was warm. More mild December weather was promised for the next several days. That's the way it often was along the coastal area of North Carolina. Tom and Willie Boy lived on the Outer Banks, a narrow ribbon of barrier islands between the mainland and the Atlantic Ocean. The Outer Banks stretched for more than a hundred miles from the Virginia-North Carolina border southward. The islands were shaped like a rather skinny right arm, with the hand up toward Virginia and the elbow—Cape Hatteras—sticking out into the Atlantic.

John Livermore didn't say anything before stepping off the porch and coming toward Tom. Willie Boy stopped grinning and stood quietly beside Tom. As he approached, his face blank, John Livermore nodded once at Tom, but still didn't speak. Tom smiled and extended his hand, then let it drop to his side as Livermore made no effort to shake hands. Tom maintained his smile, showing a lot of teeth but otherwise his face remained almost expressionless. Willie Boy frowned at Livermore and shifted his stance.

John Livermore's wife, a faded blue sweater over her housedress, came to the front door, eyed them a moment, and without speaking went back inside.

John Livermore was a tall, big boned man, weathered, and in his fifties. Tom was almost as tall, and close to thirty years younger than Livermore.

Livermore stood in front of Tom and Willie Boy, still not speaking. With his faded gray eyes, he appeared to be appraising Tom. He ignored Willie Boy. Then he said, "Boat's around back."

The three of them walked toward the canal and the boat. A large storage shed stood on the right side of the house, about fifteen yards from the far corner of the house. From the edge of the shed they stood near the canal and the boat. "It's all gassed up. Full," John Livermore said. "Keys in the ignition." Then he turned to Tom. He eyed Tom as if he were looking completely through his skull. "You got the money?"

"Right here," Tom said, and patted his right pocket. Tom shifted his posture, ready to talk business with John Livermore, give him the instructions he had down pat. "Okay, Mr. Livermore. Tomorrow night you and your wife need to be gone."

John Livermore nodded. "We will be."

"Go to Raleigh or some place inland, spend the night at

a motel, eat a nice meal or two—and be sure to always use a credit card. Establish that you're not here and have no idea that your boat was stolen overnight." Tom saw the expression on John Livermore's face. "But that's just if something should go wrong, and I certainly don't expect anything to go wrong. If it should, though, you've got proof that you were nowhere around here." Tom tried a reassuring half-smile.

Willie Boy spoke up with a grin, "Yeah, you and your wife were away enjoying a second honeymoon."

John Livermore glared at Willie Boy a moment, not speaking, and then turned back to Tom. "The money?"

Tom tugged the bills from his pocket. He handed them to Livermore. "Twenty-five thousand," he said. "You can count it."

John Livermore gave the slightest shake of his head. "No need," he said. He clutched the bills in his big hand, squeezing the bills tight; he stuffed them deep into the pocket of the heavy twill pants he wore. Then, "We'll be gone from here before noon tomorrow."

Tom said, "We'll be here late tomorrow afternoon, just before dark." He glanced at the shed. "Park back here, out of sight?"

John Livermore nodded and turned to walk back toward the front of the house. He stopped and turned toward Tom. "Just don't get my boat shot up or nothing. Wanna see it setting right back there tied up to my dock when we get home Sunday evening, good as new."

"Yes, sir, it'll be here," Tom said. "Don't worry."

Late the next afternoon Tom and Willie Boy Applewaite drove down again toward Stumpy Point to John Livermore's to park their car behind the shed and board Livermore's boat. They wore hip-length pea coats and knit caps that could be pulled down over their ears for warmth. They had gloves stuffed in the pockets of the pea coats that they would don once out on the water. The weather was still unseasonably mild for mid-December but it would be cold in the middle of the night off shore on the ocean rendezvousing with the boat they were to meet after midnight.

Tom knew the waters well. He held a captain's license and Willie Boy had often served as first mate when they went out on fishing charters. This was not a fishing expedition. They were to meet an ocean going fifty-foot shrimp trawler. It would not be loaded with shrimp but with compacted bales of marijuana.

Tom got aboard Livermore's boat and started the twin 250-hp Yamahas, set them to idle. The engines made a comfortable, low-throated throbbing. Tom could smell the clean exhaust. He was pleased with the way the engines sounded and responded to the lightest touch of the throttle. Willie Boy untied the lines, tossed them over the gunwale and hopped aboard. Tom stood at the controls, Willie Boy at the starboard gunwale, watching carefully as they eased out of the canal and headed slightly southward before swinging around about thirty degrees with a northeast heading toward Oregon Inlet.

Willie Boy smiled big. "Nice boat," Willie Boy said. Tom nodded and stared forward.

They had a long way to go and it was already dark, with only a sliver of moon coming up over the ocean. Getting through Oregon Inlet was always tricky because of shoaling and often conflicting tides or currents. But Tom was good at it. He glanced at his watch, using the glow of the instrument panel. It would take them the better part of three hours to get to the designated coordinates in the Atlantic. With a full tank, they had plenty of fuel for the trip, but out of habit, every few minutes Tom eyed the fuel gauge, the tachometer, depth finder, and compass. Once they reached the coordinates, they would have to wait and hope that the trawler showed up and there were no problems.

At midnight they were at their spot in the Atlantic, bobbing gently with the bow meeting the low waves, rocking them. Tom kept the engine idling, and from time to time he would bump the boat back in place against the flow of the Labrador Current. They were right at the edge of the Gulf Stream and warmer water. They shared a thermos of coffee that Tom had prepared. Willie Boy shivered, flexed his shoulders as if to warm his muscles, then stepped to the side and took a leak over the gunwale.

They waited.

"Maybe they won't show," Willie Boy said.

"They'll show," Tom said. He squinted toward the southeast. The boat's bow rose and fell gently, as the swells increased a tad. On one of the rises of the bow, Tom was sure he saw the faint light of a boat approaching them in the darkness. The other boat's white light showed intermittently, as if it were clicked on and off.

"I think they're coming," Tom said just loud enough to be heard over the engine and the waves lapping against the hull.

Willie Boy leaned forward, putting his hands on the gunwale, straining to see. "Yeah," he said.

Minute by minute the little white light blinked on and off, closer and closer. Then rising out of the darkness the big trawler took shape, heading toward them. Tom had his running lights on. He clicked them off and then on again three times. The trawler slowed to a crawl, and responded by turning its running lights on and off three times. The trawler got closer and Tom and Willie Boy could see two men standing near the bow, a lone person in the cabin at the wheel. The two men held automatic carbines. They held them in a relaxed manner, but ready to go into action if they had to, and do it quickly.

The captain of the trawler began to maneuver closer to Livermore's boat, coming alongside. The two men slung their weapons across their shoulders and each picked up boat hooks as the gap between the two boats closed.

Tom told Willie Boy to help get the boats secured together. His voice tinged with nervousness, Tom said, "I've
got to go aboard their boat and speak to the captain. I wanna
make sure he knows who we are . . . and that we know who
he is."

Lines were slung from the trawler to cleats on Livermore's
boat. Tom stepped across. Neither of the two men offered a
hand. Willie Boy looked at them. The men were dark
skinned and spoke to each other in what Willie Boy assumed
was Spanish. Willie Boy kept his eyes on his brother, who
stood inside the cabin of the trawler talking to the captain.
He realized his breathing came faster and he could feel his
heart beating in his chest. His brother's conversation with the
boat captain appeared even and straightforward. From inside
his pea coat, Tom removed a thick, sealed envelope and
handed it to the captain. Tom and the captain both nodded.
They didn't shake hands, and Tom left the cabin and went
past the two guys. The captain said something to the two
men and they began to get the bales of marijuana ready to
transfer to Livermore's boat.

There were ten bales of the marijuana, compacted to
about two-by-three feet each. By the time the two men
grappled the bales over to Tom and Willie Boy and they had
them stowed away, they were all four sweating. Tom and
Willie Boy pulled a tarp loosely over the last two bales. The
two men on the trawler never returned any of Willie Boy's
smiles until they finished. Then the older of the two gave a
quick smile, showing a gold tooth that caught a glow from
the Livermore's running lights. The lines were quickly
untied, tossed back to the trawler, which was already gunned
and speeding away as the lines landed on its deck.

By five o'clock that morning, Tom had motored Livermore's

boat inbound beyond Oregon Inlet and into a deep creek on
the west side of Roanoke Island, north of Wanchese. He cut
the engine and waited. He and Willie Boy scanned the brush
and undergrowth on each side of the creek. Within two minutes, a flashlight beam blinked on three times, and two men
stepped out of the underbrush to the lip of the creek. Willie
Boy recognized them and they exchanged grins.

"All okay?" Tom said.

Barely above a whisper, one of the two young men said,
"Yep." He displayed a cell phone. "I've already called. Two
trucks be here in no more'n five minutes. Want a get unload-
ing that stuff?"

"We'll wait a couple minutes," Tom said. "But help us
get over to the bank there." Tom trimmed the engines up almost out of the water.

Willie Boy tossed two lines to the men and they pulled
the boat flush against the bank, the keel brushing lightly
against the sandy bottom of the creek.

One of the young men, giving Tom what passed for a
friendly smile, said, "Before we get started, you got something for us. Been here all night you know."

"Yeah, yeah," Tom said. "Let's get this stuff off the boat
and ready for the trucks, and then I'll settle with you."

To Tom, Willie Boy whispered, "How much they getting?"

"Five thousand each."

"Jesus," Will Boy breathed.

"I don't set the prices," Tom said. "They keep a lookout.
Gotta have 'em."

Willie Boy heard the two panel trucks approaching before they came into view. No headlights were on and the
trucks moved slowly across more of a sandy path than a
road. The trucks stopped a few yards from where they stood.
The drivers got out without speaking and they helped unload
the marijuana, putting half in one truck, half in the other.
Willie Boy didn't ask Tom, but he assumed the truck drivers

would be paid when they made their delivery because Tom didn't offer any money and they didn't ask for any.

It was the last bale of marijuana, the first one loaded from the trawler to Livermore's boat, and the one on the bottom of the pile that had split open.

Tom bent over it and said, "Oh, shit." To the others he called, "Let me tie this one back up. Came undone."

Willie Boy looked over Tom's shoulder. The other four stood on the bank waiting for the final bale. Willie Boy narrowed his eyes and nudged Tom and pointed. "Yeah," Tom whispered. "I see it. Don't say anything."

What Willie Boy saw were bricks of cocaine hidden inside the bale of marijuana. Tom slipped one of the bricks inside his pea coat. "Little insurance," he whispered to Willie Boy.

Willie Boy and Tom got the bale retied and passed it over to the others without comment. The retied bale was loaded into one of the trucks. The other truck was already pulling away. Neither of the drivers had said a word. The two men who served as lookouts, came to the edge of the boat, and Tom handed each of the lookouts a bundle of tightly rolled bills. The two men grinned and they waved to Willie Boy as they pushed Livermore's boat away from the bank. Tom eased it in reverse and back out into open waters. He glanced at his watch. It was six-thirty and beginning to get light. In another hour and a half they'd have John Livermore's boat docked at his place and be through.

As he pushed the throttle forward and the boat got to plane, speeding along, Tom smiled big. Like Willie Boy, he had a great smile, but just didn't use it as often as Willie Boy did. Tom turned to Willie Boy who stood beside him at the wheel. "We made good money tonight," he said, "but we're delivering cocaine. Worth a whole whale of a lot more'n pot, so I'm going to say we get more money for our deliveries."

"They gonna agree?" Willie Boy said.

"They'll have to," Tom said. "They'll have to."

Willie Boy looked at the side of Tom's face, at the set of his jaw. He felt a great love for his brother.

Chapter Two

Three Days Later

Shortly after dawn that mild December morning Benjamin Burrus sped along the Roanoke Sound toward Manteo. His twenty-one foot Grady White boat left a foamy white wake across the still waters of the sound. Burrus stood at the center console of his boat, his hands lightly gripping the wheel. Weathered and mottled by the sun, his hands appeared older than his sixty-three years. He glanced over his right shoulder toward the rising sun. Where the light from the sun touched the sound, the water was like dull, lightly hammered pewter. Being out this early, his favorite time of day, made Burrus feel good, like everything in the world was new and filled with hope. He was headed to Manteo to pick up his fishing buddy, Hamp Ferguson, and they were going to try for rock-fish near the Mann's Harbor Bridge. It promised to be a happy time.

But as he approached red channel marker number six, he saw something bulky hanging on the steel ladder of the marker.

With his right hand, he throttled back and his boat wallowed out of plane, the bow rose, then settled with hardly any forward motion as if he'd slammed on brakes.

Staring at the ladder that ran alongside the channel

marker, he said, "Oh, my God." Then he said it again.

His chest felt like it had taken a sharp thump from a powerful fist.

There hanging on the ladder was a man's body. The wrists were tied to one of the ladder's rungs. The man's jean-clad legs dangled in the water. The wet denim looked purple. The man's head lolled to one side and there was blood on the side of his head and down his neck.

Burrus nudged his boat into reverse and then quickly back to neutral. He gripped the wheel with his left hand and reached for his marine radio. His hand trembled and he fumbled with his radio, almost dropping it. He punched in 16, the Coast Guard's frequency.

"May Day," he said, his voice croaking. "May Day. May Day."

A voice crackled back over the radio asking what was the emergency.

"A dead man," Burrus said. "A dead man's tied up to buoy number six, out of Manteo."

There was a pause. Then, "Sir, a launch will be on its way. Manteo police are being alerted. They will send a unit to channel marker number six. And, sir?"

"Yes?"

"Please stay where you are. Don't leave."

Burrus had to clear his throat again to speak. "Yes, yes. I'll be here."

With a gentle breeze from the east, his boat kept drifting toward the buoy and Manteo. Repeatedly Burrus bumped the gearshift briefly into reverse to stay in position but not get too close to the body. His boat rocked gently in the light chop. He took deep breaths and every minute or so he focused his eyes on the horizon and then back to the console of his Grady White. A seagull drifted in the air currents and appeared set to land atop the channel marker; it swooped low, but just before perching, changed direction and flew away.

After a while Burrus forced himself to study more close-ly the man hanging there on the ladder. He stared quickly at the man's face, then away. Burrus believed he recognized the man. He was sure he had seen him around the county. But in death with blood on the side of his head and neck, even down to his shoulder, his head slumped to one side, Burrus couldn't be sure. Death, especially violent death, trans-formed appearances. And, besides, he didn't want to see him too closely. His gaze went back to the horizon and he took another deep, controlled breath. He realized he chewed his lower lip as he waited for the Coast Guard and the police. Everything was so calm and serene there on the water that a dead man hanging only a few yards away seemed totally in-congruous to him.

Actually it was a little more than fifteen minutes until the authorities began to arrive, although to Burrus it seemed like it took forever before he saw and then heard the Coast Guard launch from down at Wanchese approaching the buoy. The twenty-five foot launch came at full speed, a frothy wake curved out behind her. From the other direction, the Manteo police boat appeared, then another one right behind it.

Other boaters, those few out early, would have heard Burrus's radio exchange with the Coast Guard, and the curious might soon very well converge on the scene.

All three of the boats aimed straight at the buoy and then throttled back at the last moment, settling out of plane and rocking gently as they eased closer. They hung there in the water close to the channel marker. Burrus saw the expression on the faces of the young Coast Guardsmen as they peered at the body hanging on the ladder, then they cast their eyes down or away.

Dare County Chief Deputy Odell Wright, his face still creased with sleep, was in one of the police boats. He di-rected the pilot of his boat to nudge closer to the buoy. One of the officers on the police boat attached a line to the buoy and pulled the boat alongside the ladder and the body. Immediately another of the officers began taking pictures of the body, and close-ups of how the wrists were tied to the ladder. The wrists appeared tied with a plastic coated clothesline. A Coast Guardsman also took pictures. Wright used his handheld radio to converse with someone back in his office. Then Wright turned to Burrus and yelled across to him. "Did you see anyone else when you came up on the scene?"

Burrus shook his head. "No." He swallowed and tried to lick his lips. "I just saw something big hanging on the ladder. I didn't know it was . . . it was a person at first."

Deputy Wright nodded, and studied the body again. The cords around the man's wrists had cut into the flesh but there was hardly any blood.

One of the officers in the boat with Wright asked him something. Wright turned the corners of his mouth down and shook his head sadly as if he could hardly believe it, and he said, "Yes, I know who it is." He exhaled slowly, a pained expression on his face. "It's Tom Applewaite." He continued to shake his head. "I just wonder where his brother Willie Boy is."

Chapter Three

The two brothers, Tom and Willie Boy Applewaite, were so rascally charming, so full of life and mischief that I sensed the first time I met them and basked in their captivating smiles that they were marked for death.

In a way, such a premonition may seem strange. But maybe it's not so unusual. I remember that in the old war movies when the soldiers were preparing for battle, I knew right from the get-go that the freckled-faced farm boy from Iowa, the somewhat naive youngster, was going to get killed. Well, I guess it was that way in my mind with the Applewaite brothers.

It was as if death masks flickered across their faces just for an instant while we stood outside the courtroom in Manteo this past July where they had just been cleared of charges of possession with intent to distribute marijuana. It was an eerie feeling I had; not at all a comfortable one. A brush of chill moved over me. I forced it away and returned their smiles.

They bubbled with good cheer as if they had received word that lovely young girls had signaled their desire to be with them forever; they didn't act at all like they had been spared by a technicality of spending a considerable time in Dare County's lockup.

At twenty-nine, Tom was three years older than Willie

Boy. When first meeting them, Tom gave the impression as far more serious and levelheaded than Willie Boy. Willie Boy bounced with energy like a frisky puppy, a goofy grin pasted on his face. Tom had that same big smile when he used it but he simmered with a barely concealed drive and determination, an unbridled ambition that could make him dangerous to those who stood in his way—or dangerous to himself.

It was two years earlier that I first heard about the Applewaite brothers. Actually at that time I didn't know their names. I just knew that kindly Sheriff Eugene Albright and my long-time friend SBI Agent T. (for Thomas) Ballsford Twiddy had gone to Wanchese to meet with the two brothers. It was an effort on the sheriff's part to put a bit of fear into the brothers because he had learned that they were flirting with becoming involved in the drug trade. Sheriff Albright had known the brothers' late father, and he liked the two boys. He wanted to keep them out of trouble. That's the way Albright is.

It was only later, when having coffee with Sheriff Albright and Agent Ballsford Twiddy, known to his friends as Balls, that I happened to hear the brothers' names as the sheriff and Balls chatted informally about what was going on in the county. Upon hearing Albright mention the two brothers, my reporter's instincts took over and I mentally filed their names away. I figured I might run across them at some point. That's because I'm a crime writer. My name is Harrison Weaver and I've lived here on North Carolina's Outer Banks for more than three years now, after spending a decade and a half as an investigative journalist throughout the Southeast, and with much of that time in the Washington, DC, area.

Following the brief exchange with Tom and Willie Boy Applewaite that day outside the Dare County courtroom, I casually did a bit of checking on their backgrounds. It wasn't any concerted investigation on my part; just bits and pieces of information would come to my attention, and I'd store them away in little mental file drawers I tend to keep. Never know, I've learned, when a bit of information will come in handy.

Both of the brothers worked as watermen in various capacities. Tom had a captain's license and hired himself out to run charter boats out of Oregon Inlet or Wanchese and occasionally out of Pirate's Cove. He was good at it, too, everyone said. He could navigate the tricky shoals of Oregon Inlet, getting safely and successful out to sea under the Bonner Bridge when others might run aground. Usually Willie Boy served as first mate when Tom operated a boat. From time to time they had owned their own boats but generally lost them for financial reasons.

It was because of their experience with the Outer Banks' many waterways, coves, inlets, and deep creeks that I'm sure tempted the brothers' flirtation with drug trafficking—and made them especially attractive for a dealer looking for someone to help do the pickup and delivery.

I didn't know the details, but at one point Tom and Willie Boy became involved with a dealer. With Tom's ambition, I know he was not long content with being simply a paid—and well-paid—deliveryman. He wanted to become more of the boss, the big man.

And now he was dead.

Chapter Four

I was at the courthouse when they brought Tom Applewaite's body ashore.

A dark rubberized sheet covered the body. I had come out to the docks across from the courthouse and shops. Normally I wouldn't be at the courthouse that early in the morning. But like others I had planned to take advantage of the rockfish running that morning and I'd had my marine radio sitting on the kitchen counter when I was making early morning coffee and I heard the "May Day" call. I scrapped the idea of fishing and headed straight down to Manteo and the courthouse.

I stood there silently and watched. Deputy Wright nodded to me once, and went back to supervising the body. Other deputies and Manteo police kept onlookers away. Wright barked at one of the deputies and the deputy began to string crime scene yellow tape around the area. It certainly wasn't the crime scene, but it was where Tom Applewaite's body now lay.

Within a few minutes, a rumpled Dr. Willis, the coroner, appeared. He wore a grease-stained canvas-like parka over his suit coat. He struggled out of the parka, glanced around, and handed it over to a deputy who had his hand outstretched. Dr. Willis didn't have on a tie with his wrinkled dress shirt. First time I'd ever seen him without a tie. Well, still early in the day. He pulled latex gloves out of a side pocket of his coat and worked his hands into them, all the time staring down at the shrouded form in front of him. With obvious painful discomfort, Dr. Willis knelt stiffly by the body and lifted the rubberized covering to expose Tom Applewaite's neck and head. Then he studied Applewaite's wrists. Once or twice Dr. Willis shook his head, a mournful expression playing across his face.

I couldn't hear what Dr. Willis was saying to Deputy Wright, but Wright told me later that Dr. Willis estimated time of death from his preliminary examination as sometime during the night, probably close to midnight. Two bullet holes were in Applewaite, one in the back of the head and one behind his right ear. Probably small caliber. There were no exit wounds.

While Dr. Willis continued to examine the body, and apparently giving instruction that it be sent to Greenville for autopsy, I heard the screaming.

The sound was loud, almost inhuman in its intensity. It came closer and increased in volume.

The wailing, a low-pitched howl, grew closer to me.

Before I could see him, I knew who it was, who was screaming, shouted words or sounds, pierced with curses.

Deputy Wright knew who it was too. He rose quickly from where he knelt with Dr. Willis by the body. To me, Wright yelled, "Stop him."

Willie Boy Applewaite broke past two officers standing guard. Willie Boy, tears streaming down his cheeks, his eyes wild, his mouth distorted, rushed toward his brother's body. I tried to grab his arm, but he jerked it away. He stopped abruptly at the dark rubberized form. Dr. Willis had quickly covered Tom Applewaite's face.

Willie Boy stood heaving breaths in and out, his chest rising and falling, and making that moaning sound from deep inside his body. His grief changed his face. He hardly resembled the person I had seen earlier that year. His countenance had aged instantly, and was distorted not only with grief but also with anger that radiated from him.

Deputy Wright, stood erect and braced, ready to restrain Willie Boy if he needed to. I moved closer and stood behind Willie Boy.

Willie Boy froze, staring at the dark form. The moaning sound stopped and his voice was deep and level as he said, "I want to see him."

I couldn't help but wonder how he knew, and knew so quickly, that it was his lifeless brother who lay there. The word spreads with warp speed around Manteo, so I figured that . . . well, it didn't really matter. He knew, and that was all that mattered.

Wright nodded at Dr. Willis. Dr. Willis emitted a soft sigh and eased back the covering revealing Tom Applewaite's face.

Willie Boy dropped to his knees. "Oh, no, no," he wailed over and over, and he put one hand out and touched his brother's cheek. He brushed a lock of hair from Tom's forehead, patting it back in place. Willie Boy's shoulders slumped and he looked as if he might collapse; Deputy Wright put out a hand to steady him. I came closer, ready to assist if needed.

Wright cast his eyes toward me. "See if you can get him to ease back a bit."

I nodded and put a hand gently on Willie Boy's shoulder. I whispered to him, "Let's step back, Willie Boy, and let them take care of Tom."

He shook his head violently. "The sonsabitches. The sonsabitches." His jaw jutted out. "I know who did it. I'm gonna get 'em. The sonsabitches." His voice was solid and laden with anger. He stared at the form and didn't move.

I tugged lightly at the denim jacket he wore. "Come on, Willie Boy. Let's let them take care of your brother."

Slowly he began to rise.

"The authorities will get whoever did this. They'll track

them down," I said.

For the first time, Willie Boy glanced at my face. "Shit," he sneered. "I'm gonna get 'em."

Deputy Wright heard the exchange and took two long steps over to where I stood with Willie Boy. "Willie Boy, don't do anything foolish now. We'll have the best people on this. Not just local but SBI too."

Two Dare County medics stood at the ready near the body.

Willie Boy acted as though he didn't even hear Deputy Wright. "Where they taking him?"

"To Greenville. Do some more examination, gather what evidence they can."

Willie Boy made a snorting noise. "Evidence, bullshit. I don't need any evidence. I know who did it."

Wright tried a different approach. "And you can help us, Willie Boy." Wright put out a hand on Willie Boy's arm. But Willie Boy abruptly shook the hand away. Wright's face remained neutral, but he trained his eyes on Willie Boy. "Don't go doing any . . . any Lone Ranger sort of stuff. That'd be bad. Let us handle it."

For the first time, Willie Boy glanced briefly at Wright, and curled his upper lip ever so slightly but didn't say anything. Then he turned to watch the medics as they carefully moved Tom's body to a gurney with collapsible legs. The tears started again running down Willie Boy's cheeks. "I wanna go with 'em," Willie Boy said.

Deputy Wright hesitated, as if he wasn't sure what the regulations were that would prohibit or allow Willie Boy to go with the medics. "Let me ask the chief medic," Wright said and strode back to where they were loading the body. He spoke softly to the medics. They appeared doubtful, too, and studied Willie Boy, before giving a shrug of acquiescence.

Wright turned back to Willie Boy. "Okay," he said. "But they won't stay. They'll take Tom there and come on back.

You'll have to ride back with them this afternoon."

Willie Boy nodded like he agreed. I wasn't sure he did.

Wright continued: "Now listen to me, Willie Boy. You come back with them, you hear? I could take you in right now to question you about what you say about knowing who did this. But I want to give you time to, you know, compose yourself a little bit and . . . and say goodbye to your brother, but then I want to talk to you, official like."

Willie Boy watched as they put the gurney in the back of the vehicle.

"You hear me now, Willie Boy? You got to come back to the courthouse soon as you get back."

Willie Boy nodded but didn't look at Deputy Wright.

"You've got to help us—help us do our job. And you've got to stay out of it."

Without responding, Willie Boy climbed into the emergency vehicle right behind the gurney. He perched on a small stool, staring at his brother's shrouded body. A medic climbed in also and pulled the door shut behind him.

The vehicle eased away from the docks, as officers and bystanders stepped back a few paces to make a clear path for it to head west toward Greenville.

I turned to Deputy Wright. His shoulders slumped and he appeared to have aged fifteen years that morning. Creases of worry wrinkled his forehead and deep lines ran down his cheeks. The morning light caught the silvery whiskers on his coffee-colored skin. "You think Willie Boy's coming back to meet you in the courthouse?" I posed the question even though I already knew Wright's answer.

He made a clucking sound. "I doubt it." Then he firmed up his stance. "But I know how to get him, bring him in." We started moving toward the courthouse. With a sideways glance at me, he said, "Your buddy SBI Agent Ballsford Twiddy is on his way down here today."

I figured Wright made a call to Agent Twiddy shortly after Applewaite's body was discovered.

Wright puffed out a sigh. "I'll be glad to turn this over to him."

We stepped off the curb to cross the street to the court-house. No traffic was coming. We were silent a moment, and then I said, "Drugs?"

"Oh, yeah," Wright responded. "Agent Twiddy and some DEA officers are working on that angle. We know that Tom and Willie Boy were involved, making some runs for higher ups. Don't know who they are yet, but I've got a feeling we're going to find out from Willie Boy. They're the ones we want."

"Tom get crosswise with these higher ups?"

Wright stopped on the courthouse steps and rubbed a palm across the stubble of whiskers on his chin. "I think it's obvious. That was an execution hit. The boss or bosses send-ing a message that Tom somehow got out of line. Got him done in."

I kept silent.

"Now we got to worry about Willie Boy. Make sure he's not the next one."

Chapter Five

As Deputy Wright reached out to enter the courthouse, the door suddenly swung open and Ellen Pedersen, known to almost everyone as Elly, stepped onto the porch, an expression of concern on her face. Wright moved back slightly. She nodded at Wright and then turned to me.

"What a terrible thing about Tom Applewaite," she said. Two little creases of worry were there between her eyebrows.

Yes, word does travel fast at the courthouse. Elly works in the Register of Deeds office. And Elly is my sweetheart.

I glanced at my watch. I hadn't realized enough time had elapsed so that the normal workday had started.

"Did you know him?" I said, referring to Tom Applewaite.

"Oh, I knew who he was. He and his brother, Willie something. I've seen them around town and here at the courthouse. The sheriff took a real interest in them, and tried to keep them out of trouble. Both of them as charming as they could be. Those smiles could coax a bird from a tree."

Deputy Wright put his hand on the courthouse doorknob. "And, speaking of the sheriff, I gotta go shave. Up too early to do it before I came out here. But the good sheriff doesn't see that as an excuse." He gave a mirthless chuckle, and disappeared inside.

Elly turned and glanced toward the window of her office. "And I've got to get back to work, but I saw you out here." She pursed her lips and said, "Might know that you'd be on the scene."

I shrugged. "Heard it on the marine radio."

She raised an eyebrow in mock disapproval.

I changed the subject. "See you tonight?"

"I hope so." Then as she turned to reenter the courthouse, she said, "What are you going to do now?"

"Agent Twiddy is on his way here. I may hang around a while, see if I can catch him."

She made a little face that said, "Yep, you're at it again."

But it was now truly *mock* disapproval, Elly had mostly gotten over the fact that, as a crime writer, I needed to be involved. That had been a worrisome thing in the beginning of our relationship. Understandable, actually. My involvement had put us both in extreme danger—about as extreme as you can get since we damn near got killed. Something she is not about to quickly forget.

I smiled and she disappeared into the courthouse. I stood there a few minutes and then strolled across Sir Walter Raleigh Street and went upstairs to have a coffee and maybe a muffin. Sit outside at one of the tables, keep an eye on the courthouse, watching for Agent Twiddy. Friendship—and respect—for Twiddy, or Balls as I called him, dated back several years when I was a reporter and happened to run across evidence and clues that helped Balls solve a puzzling case. Since that time, he said he considered me his lucky charm. The fact that I knew when to keep my mouth shut helped in his trust of me.

I had finished my coffee and walnut muffin and continued to sit on the narrow porch of the coffee shop. A woman came out of the shop carrying a to-go cup, smiled, and said, "We've got springtime today." I agreed. The sun was out and it was more like a spring day than the middle of

December. But the weather here on the Outer Banks can change practically in the blink of an eye. And can change frequently as well. Even though it was close to seventy degrees today, the forecast called for a severe and bone-chilling drop in temperature, with brisk ocean winds out of the northeast, within a few days.

After a while I thought I heard the throaty rumble of Balls' classic Thunderbird. I was right because in a moment Balls came around to the front steps of the courthouse wearing his somewhat rumpled tan cotton sport coat with the big pockets over the top of a muted plaid shirt, no tie. I started down the steps and called to him.

He stopped and looked over. He shook his head. "Might have known it," he muttered as I approached. "Dead body, here you are."

"Good to see you, too, Balls."

"Like your good buddy DA Schweikert says, you always show up around dead bodies."

Rick Schweikert was not my favorite person; and I was certainly not his in return. The animosity dated back to a magazine piece I had done a depicting him more or less truthfully—as pompous, stuffy, and arrogant.

Balls stuck out his big paw of a hand. "Who's the lead on this?"

"Deputy Odell Wright. But I expect you are now."

He gave a sort of halfway smile that tilted his Tom Selleck mustache up on one side. "He inside?"

I nodded.

"Where's the body?"

"On the way to Greenville."

He raised his eyebrows. "Shit. Already?"

"Not much to see. Dr. Willis looked him over. Two shots in the head. Back and by the right ear. Probably small caliber. No exit."

"Execution hit. Real pros," Balls said. He made a face. "And tied up by his wrists to the buoy." He shook his head.

"Not just an execution, but a message as well." He turned and started to go in the courthouse. He paused, peered at me. "The brother? Willie Boy. Where's he?"

"He went with the body in the EMS vehicle. Greenville. Deputy Wright told him to come back to the courthouse."

That twisted half smile again. "Yeah. Fat chance."

"Willie Boy says he knows who did it and he's going to get them."

"He may think he will, but he doesn't know what he's up against."

I put my hand on Ball's big arm, hoping to detain him a moment longer. It felt like I grasped the business end of a baseball bat. "Tom and Willie Boy running drugs?"

Balls gave me one of his phony official looks. "Ongoing investigation, you know."

"Aw, come on Balls," I said.

After a beat or two, he gave a slight nod of his head and said, "We have an informant who confirms that."

"Confidential informant?" I said. "Just like TV."

Balls frowned at me, cocking one eyebrow like he thought I was getting smartass.

I changed my tone. "Tom getting too ambitious?"

Balls adjusted his jacket, stalling for time. "Okay, our guy says a bale of marijuana broke open and Tom saw there were bricks of cocaine inside. He wanted more money to be a delivery man for cocaine."

"But you don't know who the higher ups are? They're the ones you're after."

"No, we don't know. And yes, they are the ones we want to apprehend." He studied me a moment, and then said, "The number of people and money involved in an operation is mighty . . . mighty big." He held up a hand and starting raising one finger at a time. "First off, a boat to go out off-shore to meet an incoming shipment. What boat? Oh, maybe offer twenty grand or more to a boat owner to 'borrow' his boat. Tell him to take his wife inland for a weekend vacation.

Tell him to use credit cards so if something goes wrong, he can always claim his boat was stolen while he and his wife were honeymooning inland somewhere. And he can prove he was nowhere around because of the credit card charges." He held up another finger and continued. "Then they've got to have lookouts twenty-four hours a day where they plan to bring the drugs back to shore. These people got to get paid." He held up a third finger. "And then there's got to be one or two unmarked vehicles to transport the goods." He shook his head, and with a dismissal wave of his hand, said, "Lots of people involved, and many of them never done anything like this." He gave a phony chuckle. "When commercial fishing gets slow, not too hard to recruit some help."

"Isn't the DEA involved in this?"

"Sure, but not the murder. That's ours—SBI and Dare County."

"I haven't seen any DEA agents around," I said.

Balls cocked his head at me, a wry smile playing around his mouth. "Yeah you have seen 'em. You just didn't know they were DEA."

I realized that might very well be true. Then, hoping I could get him to stay a moment longer, I said, "The head man? Where's he operating from? New York? Philadelphia? Washington?"

He gave a dismissive snort and twisted the knob on the courthouse door. "Would you believe right here on the Outer Banks? From what we think, it's someone no one would suspect . . . but we haven't pinned it down yet, not by a long shot. So keep that info under your hat, or someplace. Don't let it get out." He pulled open the door and grinned at me. "Don't even tell your sweetie."

He stepped inside and was gone. Well, I got a whole lot more out of him than I thought I would.

It was still early for lunch, and I had eaten the muffin, but I figured that by the time I went back across the Roanoke Sound to the Bypass, I would stop at Capt'n Frank's Hot

Dogs and get a foot-long and cheese fries, topping it off with a Diet Dr. Pepper. My comfort food. Later I would call Rose Mantelli, my New York editor (with a heavy Brooklyn accent) to tell her there's another murder down here in Magnoliaville, as she refers derisively to my home, her remark almost always punctuated by a laugh and cigarette-induced cackling.

Crossing over Washington Baum Bridge, high above the sound, the sun sparkled on peeks of gentle waves. But despite the beautiful sunshine and mildness of the weather, I couldn't shake from my mind what Benjamin Burrus had run across earlier today—Tom Applewaite strung up on channel marker number six with two bullet holes in his head. As I have a tendency to do as a writer, I tried to picture how that all came about. Tom had to have been lured away from Willie Boy, probably set up so he didn't expect something. There had to be two or three thugs that took him out into the sound. How did they threaten him, force him to get in position so they could tie his wrists to the ladder? I don't know, of course, but I'm sure he was tied up before he was shot; be very difficult to tie him up after he was dead, but not impossible. From blood patterns, it could be determined that he was trussed up and then shot, not shot elsewhere and taken there. Maybe it's not such a stretch to figure that maybe they told him he was only going to be punished for trying to muscle in by being tied up there for an hour or two, his legs dangling in the bone-chilling waters. But then they shot him, as they'd planned all along. Or been ordered to do.

Suddenly I had to brake hard for the stoplight at Outer Banks Hospital. I'd better pay more attention to my driving.

But then I thought about the distraught Willie Boy, vowing to get the sonsabitches who did that to his brother. Okay, I know I'm a crime writer, a reporter, and not supposed to get involved in investigations—as Elly has reminded me frequently—but just the same, I shared some of Willie Boy's passion.

I wanted to get the sonsabitches also.

Chapter Six

Young Harvey greeted me at Capt'n Frank's. It was early and there were a couple of booths empty so I placed my order and sat in one of the booths, studying the pictures on the wall. Anything to quit thinking about murder and mayhem. In addition to shots of people around the globe wearing Capt'n Frank's T-shirts, there was an old one, now somewhat faded, of a visiting Johnny Cash and another of tennis star John McEnroe.

Not thinking about murder and mayhem didn't last long, though. Harvey came over to the booth with my order and said something about Tom Applewaite being murdered. Yes, the word travels fast. Harvey knew I wrote about things like that. I agreed it was a damn shame. I asked if he knew Tom and Willie Boy. Not really, he said, but he knew who they were. They came in from time to time, like most locals and tourists as well. They were always smiling and friendly with everyone.

When I left Capt'n Frank's, I drove south to my place off the Bypass, pulled in under the carport and sat there a moment or two. My little house is on a cul-de-sac and is secluded by a large live oak tree and a vacant lot on one side, another house on the other, obscured partially by a couple of scraggly pines and a large bush of some kind. Don't know what that bush is but it keeps growing and I've cut it back several times.

I sighed, got out of my Outback and trudged up the out-side steps to my kitchen door, the primary entrance to the house, which sits on stilts, like so many of the beach boxes. It's painted a light blue and I really like it.

As I opened the door, Janey, my parakeet, began chirp-ing a greeting. Happy to have company. She did her little head-bobbing dance and I spoke to her. I've had her for four years now, and although females are not supposed to mimic words, she's picked up two of them from the repeated mut-tering I've done while practicing the bass fiddle. She says those two words perfectly: "shit" and "bitch." Great vocabu-lary. I hadn't realized I repeated them so often until she began to say them. Well, trying to master some of the bow-ing techniques on Mozart's "Requiem" will do that to you.

I stepped over the neck of my bass as it lay on its side on the floor, and checked Janey's food and water, then gave her a small sprig of millet seed as a treat.

Suddenly feeling very tired, I sat on the sofa, staring at the floor. The business about Willie Boy worried me. Debat-ing with myself, I gave up and decided to call Balls on his cell. Didn't care whether he got miffed or not.

On the second ring he gave a gruff, "Yeah?"

"Been thinking about Willie Boy," I said, "and with the way he was spouting off, I figure maybe protective custody for him before he gets himself killed, too."

Balls broke in before I could continue. "You're behind the curve, Weav. I've already got Ray, the agent over in Greenville, picking him up, make sure Willie Boy gets his ass back here."

"Protective custody?"

"Don't know whether he'll stand still for that but I do know he'll stand still in custody until I get through question-ing him."

"You think he actually does know the higher up, the big guy, who killed Tom—or had it ordered?"

"Had it ordered is more like it. Don't think the top guy—whoever he is—dirties his hands. He's got heavies who do that sort of thing." Then Balls paused and I sensed he was deciding how much more he could say to me. "My guy—my informant—claims none of them—the peons, the drivers, lookouts, deliverymen, the boaters, truck drivers— none of them know who the head man is. They take their orders from someone down the line. And in this kind of operation, there are a lot of them involved. We'll get to them eventually, but it's the head honcho we want."

I was surprised I could keep Balls talking this long, and I didn't want to let him go. "And a local head man? Not Washington, New York or even Richmond?"

"Word is, a local."

"Well, if your informant or any of the others don't know, I doubt if Willie Boy actually knows . . ."

"He may know more than he thinks. I'll find out."

"By tomorrow, Balls, I'd like to meet with you and—"

"Maybe. But my job ain't to help you write those . . . those stories you write."

"Crap, Balls. I just want to—"

"Gotta go." He disconnected.

As I said, I got him talking more than I thought I would. And I assumed he would spend the night in Manteo at the Elizabethan Inn. Maybe he would agree to breakfast in the morning. He was big on breakfast, and if I offered to pay . . .

The weariness sucked back over me again. I stood slumped near Janey's cage. "Hell with it, Janey. I'm going to take a nap."

She chirped and bobbed her head.

When I piled out this morning—golly, it was just this morning—I hadn't made the bed. I kicked off my shoes and sprawled across the bed fully dressed, bunched up a pillow under my head and one shoulder and went sound asleep in short order.

It was close to two o'clock when I awakened, feeling

groggy and stiff. Shuffling into the kitchen I put on a pot of coffee. I realized I still had my windbreaker on. Decided to keep it on and take a cup of coffee out on the deck. Hell with it, I'd light a cigar too. Call my editor? Nope. I'd wait until tomorrow.

The weather was still beautiful and mild. Lots of Carolina-blue sky, only a few high, puffy clouds coming in from the southeast. I sat on one of my webbed lawn chairs I have on the deck, my coffee mug on the wrought iron table that looks so sturdily out of place between the Kmart-special chairs. Oh, well, I'm not supposed to be an interior decorator. I'd leave that to Elly if she and I ever do get married. I puffed on my cigar and told myself I was lucky to be alive, and I believed it too. I began to feel better.

And I thought about Elly. We were definitely considered a couple by those who knew us. As for marriage, we'd never come right out and talked about it. We've both been married before, but both of our spouses had died. Elly was married to a classical cellist she met while attending Meredith College in Raleigh. He was rather sickly, even in the beginning, and died within a year and a half of their marriage of a particularly virulent flu-like virus. Elly kept her maiden name of Pedersen, even though they had a son, Martin, now almost five years old. He has gotten so he will speak to me on occasion.

My wife? I say she died. I have a difficult time, still, in saying that she committed suicide. She was a musician, too, a vocalist with a great, throaty jazz voice. I played with some of the groups she sang with. But then she began to sink into depression where no one could reach her. It got worse and worse and then there was that morning I came in and found the empty pill container and she was curled up in the bed and I put my hand on her and I knew immediately she was dead. It was like touching something inanimate that had never, ever, been alive.

Afterward I went through a bad, blurred period of drinking, so that now I'm afraid to even drink a beer or a glass of wine.

Sitting there in the afternoon sunshine, I shook all those thoughts away, and decided it was time to call Elly. Get my thinking back to the here and now and happier days. When she came on the line, I asked her if she'd like to go out to eat. She urged me to come have dinner at her house. She said she wanted to make it an early evening and spend time, too, with Martin. "Mother's grilling pork chops," she said, "along with stewed apples, and I know you like that."

"I'm sold," I said. "That's awfully nice."

"See you about six," she said.

I took a quick shower and dressed in khakis and button-down soft cotton shirt, boat shoes and even socks. I grabbed my windbreaker, checked on Janey, and left a lamp on in the living room. Don't like to come back to a dark house. Traffic was light along the Bypass there at midweek, in December, despite the fact that technically it was "rush hour." While we called it the Bypass—actually it was Route 158 or Croatan Highway—and it "bypassed" nothing. Businesses flanked both sides. It ran north and south, more or less parallel to the Beach Road, the only other north-south road along this strip of the islands. The lighter traffic in the winter, plus frequent mild days like this one, were part of the joy of living on the Outer Banks, the barrier islands with the Atlantic on one side and various sounds on the other.

Elly and her mother's house is on the west side of Manteo, not far from the airport. It takes me about twenty-some minutes to drive there this time of year. Although it was not completely dark when I left my house, night was coming on fast and when I crested the Washington Baum Bridge, I could see lights on at Pirate's Cove and a glow of light from Manteo. I drove slowly through town and beyond the business section I turned left off Highway 64 and then took another left a short distance later, easing into the little road to Elly's. Her house, an original 1930s Sears structure ordered from their catalog and updated over the years, is neat and comfortable. The front yard is dominated on the left by a huge live oak, it's massive limbs creating a canopy under which Martin and his next door friend, little Lauren, play. Elly's older model Pontiac was in the gravel driveway, along with her mother's Ford.

As usual, Elly came out on her front porch to greet me with a raised hand, fingers wiggling. It was now dark and the porch light was on. I cut the engine and stepped out of the car, a smile on my face at the sight of her. She returned the smile. Stepping onto the low front porch, I gave Elly a discreet hug and a peck on her lips. She had changed clothes from those she wore at work; a bit more comfortable now: cotton light blue long-sleeve blouse, off-white jeans, sockless loafers. I love looking at her hips in slacks or jeans.

We went inside where Martin lay sprawled on the floor doodling in a coloring book, drawing stick figures it appeared.

"Say hello to Mr. Weaver, Martin," Elly said.

He gave me a quick glance and mumbled something.

"Nice drawings there, Martin," I said.

He ignored me.

I could smell supper being cooked and it was delightful. One of Elly's finished crosswords was under a lamp at the sofa's end table. Par for the course. She admits to being addicted to them.

Mrs. Pedersen came from the kitchen into the living room. "Welcome," she said. "Supper will be ready directly." She is taller than Elly, and just as trim; Mrs. Pedersen is ramrod straight with short, steel-gray hair she brushes back rather severely. From pictures I've seen of the late Mr. Pedersen, Elly takes more after her father. Her features are delicate; her dark brown hair is often pulled up exposing the fair skin of her neck. And I like looking at that, too.

"Smells awfully good," I said.

To Elly, Mrs. Pedersen said, "Have you told him about

your new part-time job yet?"

"Mother! No, I was going to surprise him."

"What's this?" I said. "What part-time job?"

"The Christmas Shop," Mrs. Pedersen said, beaming.

"Now, Mother, no surprise left . . ."

"Yes," I said, "that is *too* a surprise."

Elly put her hand on my arm, head tilted to the side. "Just weekends, and just for the Christmas rush here in December." She smiled proudly. "I'll be a salesperson in the jewelry room with Tina. And you know how I love the Christmas Shop. I'll work nine-thirty to closing Saturdays and Sundays—starting this weekend. It'll be just for this month, and it'll be fun.

"Well, that's fine. Congratulations," I said, trying to capture and return the enthusiasm she and her mother displayed.

Elly studied my face. "I'd thought about it before, and I mentioned it to Mother, and she just *happened* to run into Mr. Greene at the shop, and well, he's known me since I was a child and of course he's known Mother since *The Lost Colony* days when she had a bit part as a youngster. I went in for a quick interview at lunch, and . . . well, one thing led to another." She took a deep breath, a big smile on her face.

Again I nodded and said, "Congratulations." And I did give a big smile and I was happy she was so happy about it.

It was easy to share the affection they felt about the Island Gallery and Christmas Shop, its full name today. It has been a fixture on the Outer Banks since 1967 when Edward Greene opened it—probably one of the first of its kind in the nation. And what a unique story about its beginning—and continuation. Eddie Greene (he's still known as Eddie to his many friends) first came to the Outer Banks as a young professional dancer from New York to appear in Paul Greene's long-running outdoor drama—*The Lost Colony* —that told the intriguing story of Sir Walter Raleigh's ill-fated attempt at the first English settlement in the New

World. One hundred seventeen men, women, and children had arrived on Roanoke Island in 1587. The first child of English parentage, Virginia Dare, was born soon after their arrival. Additional supplies were supposed to be delivered the next year, but Queen Elizabeth I was involved with warding off the Spanish Armada, and she permitted no ships to sail to the struggling colony. It was three years before another ship arrived. Nothing was found of the colony except the remnants of an earthen fort and the word "Croatoan," the name of an Indian tribe, carved on a tree. No further trace of the "lost colony" has ever been found.

Nightly during the summer, *The Lost Colony* theatrical performance attracts thousands of viewers. Many of the local people have had roles in the drama over the years. Perhaps the most well known of the cast members was Andy Griffith, who as a young man played Sir Walter Raleigh. At the same time Greene, in addition to being a dancer, had the role of Uppowac, a native American.

After his stint with the show, Eddie Greene traveled around the country with Broadway productions, but his heart never left the Outer Banks, and he subsequently returned to open the Christmas Shop, which his friend, the late Andy Griffith told Eddie was a "crazy idea." But it turned out not to be so crazy after all, and it soon became a popular destination place on the Outer Banks.

Smiling, I said to Elly, "So you start work there this weekend."

She shrugged but couldn't keep from sparkling with pleasure. "It'll only be for the Christmas season."

Mrs. Pedersen hurried back to the kitchen and called over her shoulder, "We'll eat in about three minutes."

Martin had taken in the conversation. With a look of concern, he angled his head upward toward his mother. "You working there mean we don't get to play Putt-Putt on Saturday?"

"Well, Martin, I don't think any of the Putt-Putt places

are open this time of year."

"I'll see if I can find one," I said, "and on a Saturday or Sunday Martin and I will go play."

"You'd like that, wouldn't you, Martin?" Elly said.

He eyed me a moment, then nodded solemnly.

The meal was excellent, as always. The pork chops were done to perfection—not overcooked. The spiced apples added to the meal, along with fluffy mashed potatoes. By the end of the meal I said what I'd said before: "I don't see how the two of you ladies stay so slim."

Mrs. Pedersen beamed at the compliment.

Before I left that evening, the subject of Tom Applewaite came up only briefly, although I knew the specter of his murder hung there over our heads. Mrs. Pedersen brought it up, how horrible it was, but then we three studiously refrained from talking about it further.

However, as Elly and I stood on the front porch to say goodnight, with only the light coming from the living room illuminating us, she said, "I suppose your friend Agent Twiddy is in town."

"Yes, he'll be on the case, I'm sure."

Even in the dim light I could see the faux stern expression: "Just remember it is *his* case."

"Oh, no problem," I said, and leaned over and gave her a kiss goodnight. It began to develop into more than a kiss goodnight as I held her against me. I could feel her breath coming more rapidly. After a moment or two we reluctantly parted.

"Oh, boy," she said with a smile. I didn't want to part from her. I kept my hands on her waist, and then began to let them drift downward to rub her hips. "I hate to let you go, Harrison, but . . ."

"I know," I said. I stepped down to the first step, looked back at her, and said softly, "You're right with 'Oh, boy.'" I nodded my head in appreciation, smiled, and left.

Chapter Seven

Elly knew as well as I did that I'd not be able to stay out of the investigation of Tom Applewaite's death. I'd be poking my nose in, bugging Balls about what was going on. And, too, I was fully aware of the volatility exhibited by Willie Boy Applewaite. It was not idle bravado on his part when he vowed to get the sonsabitches who killed his brother. But I knew that Willie Boy would hardly be a match for the professional heavies who murdered Tom and strung him up on the channel marker.

When I got home I checked the time and figured maybe it wasn't too late to call Balls, see how things went with Willie Boy.

Two rings on his cell phone and he said, "Don't you know I'm trying to get some rest. Bedtime. Whadda you want?"

"Sorry Balls but I thought you'd be watching a rerun of *Law and Order*. Not all that late."

"Seen all the reruns." He sounded like he shuffled to sit upright. "Anything up or you just want to keep me from my beauty rest?"

"How did it go with Willie Boy today?"

"You know, same as I know, none of your damn business."

"Aw, come on, Balls."

He chuckled. "Okay. That young fella's a piece of work if there ever was one. Start with, I can't get him to agree to any sort of protection. Could take him into custody, but I've got nothing really to hold him on."

"You know he was delivering . . ."

"Knowing and proving ain't the same thing."

"So what's he doing? Running around loose?"

"We're trying to keep an eye on him, if you know what I mean."

"What about the business of going to get the killers who did that to his brother?"

"He claims he was just being emotional at the time."

"You believe him?"

"Hell, no."

"Going to play it alone?"

"Afraid so."

"Cripes, Balls. Isn't there something can be done?"

Balls sighed loudly. "Look, Weav, you stick to that typewriter of yours and . . . and play that cello with your rock 'n' roll band and let me handle police work. Okay?"

"It's a bass, not a cello, and it's a jazz combo, not rock 'n' roll."

"Whatever." He chuckled, knowing he'd got me again.

I gave a short laugh. "And it's a computer keyboard, not a typewriter. Haven't used a typewriter in years—but I still miss them."

The tone of his voice changed, got more serious. "Okay, I'm worried about Willie Boy, too. Can't help but like the scoundrel, and feel for him. And frankly, I'm afraid for him. But he claims he doesn't know anything about who the top guy is, the one we want." I could picture Balls sitting on the side of the bed, shaking his big head. "We're going to keep an eye on him as discreetly as we can, but that's about all we can do . . . and he's damn good at disappearing."

"I don't think he's through," I said.

"Neither do I." There was a pause and I sensed there

was something else on his mind. "Okay, now that you've disturbed my rest, I'm gonna run this past you."

"Yes?"

"I'm toying with the idea of you meeting with my CI—confidential informant."

"Me? Me meeting with your CI?"

"Yeah, you. Who you think I'm talking to?" His voice got softer, a bit less of the gruffness in it. He said, "But I don't know, Weav. It's just something I've been running through my mind. It'd have to be all unofficial. And it could be kind of . . . well, not dangerous or anything. Usually I see him when he—quote—has a doctor's appointment in Elizabeth City, and I happen to be at the doctor's office same time. Once or twice we've just *happened* to run into each other at Frog Island Seafood. Have to be careful he doesn't get compromised."

"I understand," I said. It was obvious where Balls was going with this and I admit I was intrigued.

"With this Tom Applewaite thing going on, it'd be a lot more convenient if I could meet him here on the Outer Banks," Balls said. "He's good, but a little, well, off center and occasionally strung out. He says only recreational drugs. Yeah, sure." He took a breath, paused again. "He plays guitar, or at least says he does. And I thought maybe if he sat in with your group for a rehearsal or something, and . . ."

"This won't put *him* in danger? You showing up?"

"I wouldn't show up. Point is, and I don't want to get you involved in a way that could backfire, but maybe you could talk with him during a rehearsal and pass that information on to me."

"Why would he talk to me?"

"Because I'd tell him to."

"Balls, you know I'll do what you'd like me to do but . . ." The idea of being more involved excited me, yet I wasn't sure this approach he was suggesting would work.

He sighed. "I'm tired. Maybe not thinking straight. This

idea of mine might be some of my end-of-the-day thinking, which ain't ever all that reliable. May be a screwy idea. Forget it for the time being. Let me sleep on it . . . if I can still get back to sleep after you've harassed me." He forced a chuckle.

"Breakfast tomorrow?" I suggested.

"Why not? Early, though. Seven-thirty. Meet halfway. The Dunes?"

"Sounds good. Seven-thirty." Then I said, "And get some sleep. Stay off the phone."

"Screw you," he said, and disconnected.

I sat there a few minutes thinking about the possibility of meeting with his informant. I wasn't sure it would work, especially since a lot of people are aware that Balls and I know each other. I wasn't convinced that Balls thought it was such a good idea either. Probably, as he said, an end-of-the-day idea. They're rarely the best. As my father used to say, never make a decision after midnight. And "end-of-the-day" was after midnight.

The next morning by seven-fifteen I drove south on the Bypass to the Dunes restaurant. It's on the east side of the highway at Whalebone Junction. Pulling into the parking area, I scouted around for Balls' Thunderbird. Well, got there before he did. Good for me. But he arrived before I got out of my car, and backed into a space beside me.

"Thought I'd give you enough time to mosey on down," he said, lumbering out of his low-slung classic car. He wore his tan cotton sport coat again. It was a bit rumpled but it covered the big sidearm he carried in a holster on his belt. It was a Glock, and not a 9mm but a serious .45 caliber. He once said, "If I have to shoot somebody, I wanna make sure he goes down . . . and stays down."

We went inside and were shown to a booth about halfway back along the windows. The hostess was young and pretty and wearing knee-length shorts and a Dunes T-shirt hanging loose.

As we sat, with Balls facing the front, he said, "Just can't help eyeing the gals, can you?"

"Admiration," I said, adding, "and shorts here in December. Got to love the Outer Banks."

We had hardly ordered breakfast—a hearty one—and sipped on the coffee when Balls, with a startled expression clouding his face, said, "Uh-oh."

I started to turn around to see what it was, but Balls shook his head just enough to stop me. Then his face went bland and neutral and he pretended to be concentrating on his coffee cup.

Someone slouched toward our booth after waving off the hostess. He passed by and sat at the booth directly behind us, his back to Balls' back, separated by the booth's low partition. He was a scruffy looking young man, not more than thirty, but it was difficult to tell because his hair was scraggly and unkempt. He had a wispy goatee and a snake-like tattoo that ran up the left side of his neck. The collar of his greasy windbreaker hid the bottom of the tattoo. He appeared to be breathing with quick gasps. The waitress approached him, a hint of concern on her face as she tried to smile. "Just coffee," he said. "Just coffee."

As though speaking to his cup, Balls said, "What are you doing here?"

"I'm spooked, Mr. Twiddy. Spooked." He spoke softly but his voice was urgent and high-pitched.

"You're using again." It wasn't a question.

The waitress brought his coffee, and asked if there was something else. He gave a quick, jerky shake of his head, and she nodded and went back to her station.

"You know better than to show up here," Balls said. "How'd you find me?"

The man took a noisy gulp of his coffee. "I asked around. Then I saw your car out front."

Balls shook his head.

The man glanced around the restaurant, which was practically empty, as if he thought someone might be hiding from him. His voice quivered, almost a sob. "I think I'm made, Mr. Twiddy. I think I'm made."

I had already figured the young man was Balls' confidential informant, and he was obviously terrified.

Balls didn't answer him. Instead, Balls slipped his cell phone from his belt and punched in a number. He spoke softly. "Odell, this is Agent Twiddy. I'm sending someone down to the courthouse to see you. Keep an eye on him." Balls listened to Deputy Odell Wright's voice, and then said, "No, not protective. Just keep him under wraps—and safe—until I get there, very shortly."

Balls put away his cell. Without turning toward the man behind him, Balls said, "Go to the courthouse, sheriff's office, and see Chief Deputy Odell Wright. He'll be looking for you."

"He's not booking me or anything, is he?"

"No. Just sit with him until I get there."

"I'm really spooked. I think they're after me."

"I told Deputy Wright to keep you safe. When I get there we'll figure out what's next. But you don't need to be around me. Not here."

I heard the young man put down several coins. Then he fished out a wadded dollar bill and added to the change. He stood and surveyed the restaurant again. Balls kept his gaze at his breakfast plate, now a bit cold. With a jerky stride as if he couldn't make his legs do right, the man moved to the front and out the door. Balls barely glanced at him as he exited. I saw a small Nissan pickup truck, an older one, pull out of the parking area and head toward the causeway and Manteo.

He didn't make it to the sheriff's office.

Chapter Eight

Reports of witnesses varied. One couple said it was a black SUV, maybe a Cadillac Escalade. Another witness swore it was a dark blue, heavy-duty pickup truck. Witnesses did agree that there were two men in the vehicle that rammed the smaller Nissan truck and forced it off the road just beyond Little Bridge, where it crashed into a large metal trash container, and that someone in the larger vehicle fired multiple times at the Nissan's driver. The gunshots sounded like a machine gun, they all agreed. There were four bullet holes in the driver's door; the driver's window was shot out, and so was half of the windshield.

The driver of the Nissan was dead, with at least three bullet holes in his upper body. One of the shots went into the snake-like tattoo on his neck.

We hadn't sat at our booth in the Dunes restaurant more than five minutes, neither of us speaking, before Balls' cell phone chirped. He had been only picking at his food, totally unlike him. I had waited for him to speak. He wouldn't look at me. Into his cell phone he said, "Yeah?"

I watched his face and I knew it wasn't good.

"Shit," he said. "I'm on my way." He rose abruptly. "Get the check," he said. He took a quick gulp from his water glass. "A shooting on the causeway. Little Bridge." He shook his head. "I think I know who." A real look of distress, as if he were to blame. "Christ," he muttered, his voice low and sad.

With quick strides he was gone.

Standing, I signaled the waitress for the check, and watched through the window as Balls sped out of the parking lot, tires burning. He'd slapped a flashing blue light on the roof of his Thunderbird and I'm sure another one pulsated in the grille. With hardly a pause, Balls raced his car out on to the Bypass, headed for the causeway. The young waitress approached, a worried look on her face, as if she'd had her quota of strange customers for the day. "Everything all right?" she asked.

"Fine, fine," I said and peeled off enough money to pay her and leave a healthy tip. I started toward the exit.

"Your jacket," the waitress called.

"Oh, thanks." I doubled back and snatched my windbreaker from the seat, putting it on as I hurried out to my car.

Traffic was light, but unlike Balls, I waited until there was a break between oncoming cars. I headed for the causeway and Little Bridge.

A short distance beyond Whalebone Junction I could see the police activity up ahead. When I crossed Little Bridge, and there was no oncoming traffic, I did what was probably illegal and pulled over to the left and parked there on the approach to a public parking area. Across the highway two Nags Head police vehicles were there, lights flashing. A Dare County Sheriff's Department cruiser had nosed in also. Deputy Odell Wright emerged from the cruiser. Balls' Thunderbird, the light on its roof still going strong, was squeezed in between two of the police cars. I got out of my Subaru and stood on the far side of the road, watching. Siren going and lights blazing, a Dare County ambulance from Manteo zoomed high across the Washington Baum Bridge, slowed momentarily, then inched its way among the growing number of vehicles at the scene. A uniformed officer stood in the middle of the highway, directing traffic and keeping it moving.

I had to walk several yards to my left, toward the Roanoke Sound and bridge—still on the opposite side of the road—before I could see the center of activity. And then I saw it: the older model Nissan truck, the one Balls' informant was driving. I couldn't see inside the cab because Balls and two officers stood near the driver's door. They were joined by Deputy Odell Wright. I knew what they were looking at. I knew there was a body slumped behind the steering wheel, the man who told Balls he was spooked.

He was right when he said he was made. Now it was all over for him.

Balls moved away from the Nissan and began what appeared to be an urgent conversation on his cell phone. From the witness accounts, the officers knew the assailants had continued toward Manteo after the attack. I assumed Balls was ordering roadblocks at each of the two bridges leading westward to the mainland. It made sense to trap the killers on Roanoke Island, if possible.

Balls spoke to Deputy Wright, then slung himself into his car; Wright got quickly into the Dare County cruiser. With lights flashing, they both spun out of the cluster of vehicles to the Washington Baum Bridge toward Manteo, leaving the other officers and the EMT crew there with the body.

I knew Balls and Wright would be looking for the assailants and the vehicle they used, the one I learned later that witnesses described as a black Cadillac Escalade or a dark blue big pickup truck, and especially one with undoubtedly a damaged right side from ramming the Nissan.

I wanted to follow Balls and Wright onto Roanoke Island, but I'd have to wait until the officer in the middle of the highway cleared traffic. Soon there was a break in the traffic and—despite getting an angry shout from the traffic officer—I managed to get onto Highway 64 near the foot of the bridge, and headed toward Manteo. There was no way I could catch up with Balls and Wright, but I figured I'd drive around and see if perhaps . . . and voila! As I started up Sir Walter Raleigh Street toward the waterfront, there were Balls and Wright with their vehicles blocking the road, lights flashing. They were out of their cars and approaching a haphazardly parked, abandoned black SUV. It was nose in at the curb, the rear end halfway into the street. I was sure, too, that it had a damaged right side.

Parking a half a block away, I scurried up to where they were. The vehicle was a Dodge Journey. Using his handkerchief, Balls opened the driver's door. I saw him sniffing and shaking his head. The steering wheel and interior had been wiped down with what was probably motor oil. An oil soaked rag lay on the floorboard. I could smell the oil, too, as I got closer. Both Balls and Wright ignored me, and I tried to stay out of their way.

Balls went to the passenger side of the Dodge. I saw him looking at the damage to the right front fender and side panel. Using his handkerchief again, he opened the door, bent down and examined something on the floorboard. I moved closer. Balls used a ballpoint pen to pick up a shell casing, drop it in a plastic bag Wright handed him. There were at least three other casings, and he did the same thing. He sniffed them and studied them closely. "Wiped clean," he said under his breath.

Wright was on his cell phone. I heard him requesting a deputy to secure the SUV. Into the phone he said, "And it's likely stolen." He gave the license number to the person on the line.

Balls continued shaking his head. "They could be anywhere now," he muttered. "Parked here, switched vehicles, and took off." He glanced at the houses bordering the street. A woman stood on one of the porches watching them. Balls hurried over to her and stood on the lower steps of her porch. She made a gesture that indicated she hadn't seen anything.

Balls came back to the vehicle. A few cars were backed

up, not able to get by. To Wright, Balls said, "Get another deputy over here to question other residents, see if they saw someone switching cars. And anything else they might have seen."

"Yes, sir."

Balls appeared to notice me for the first time. "How about staying here until the other deputy arrives. Don't let anybody mess with this vehicle. We still just might find a fingerprint."

"Sure," I said.

Then again to Wright he said, "Let's scout around town and out on the highway, toward Wanchese too. See if we run across something . . . but, hell, we don't even know what we're looking for." He made a face and puffed out a big sigh. "For all we know, they could have driven right back past the scene there at Little Bridge, taking a look at their handiwork."

Wright said, "They knew what they were doing."

"Real pros," Balls said.

Balls and Wright drove off in their separate cars, and the stalled traffic began to move again on Sir Walter Raleigh Street, even though there had to be a bit of give and take as they maneuvered around the rear end of the Dodge. I didn't think Balls and Wright would find anything any more than they thought they would. I stayed with the vehicle until a young deputy I know named Dorsey arrived. He managed to park nose-to-nose at the Dodge. He got out of his cruiser and walked to the back, checked the license plate. "Yeah, it's stolen," he said. "It was reported about an hour ago." He bobbed his head to the west. "Right out of a driveway over in Mother Vineyard, a mile or so from here."

I continued to stand there with Dorsey. Not more than fifteen minutes later, as if by prearrangement, Balls and Wright returned. Balls shaking his head as he unfolded his bulk out of the Thunderbird. The light was not flashing any longer and he took it off the roof, stored it inside behind his seat. Wright gave a brief shake to his head also, then spoke to Deputy Dorsey, who stood sentinel-like by the stolen and now abandoned Dodge Journey.

I heard Wright say to Dorsey, "Well, we've got road-blocks at both bridges here . . ."

"And at Wright Memorial, too," Balls added.

Dorsey, maybe trying to appear eager, said, "What are they going to be looking for? At the roadblocks?"

Balls gave him a look. "Something suspicious. Two guys. Probably in a late model car. Not little old ladies." Then as much to himself as the three of us, Balls said, "I'm going back to the scene at Little Bridge. Maybe there's something there that'll give us something—anything—to go on." He sounded absolutely weary, worn out, depressed.

"They moved fast and like clockwork, didn't they?" I said to Balls.

He appeared to mull something over in his mind. "I don't believe they were from here. Real hit men brought in to do a job." He clenched his fists. "I just want to know who ordered it. I want to know who's behind all of this." I saw a sadness cloud his face. Staring into my eyes, he said softly, "I wish I had been able to do more to save him, not let him get killed." I knew he referred to the scraggly, nervous young man I'd seen only briefly there in the Dunes. But Balls had been working with him for some time. And for just a moment, after he said that, I thought Balls' eyes moistened up.

Then his face changed; he jutted out his chin and said, "What worries me, too, is that it may not be over yet."

As soon as he said that, I thought of Willie Boy Apple-waite, and I wondered where he was and what he was up to.

I watched Balls drive away toward Highway 64 and Little Bridge and I felt sorry for him because he was my friend and I knew how he was feeling now.

Chapter Nine

Checking my watch, I thought about driving up another couple of blocks to see Elly at the courthouse. Decided against it. Instead, I eased into a driveway a few yards ahead of me, backed out, and headed in the opposite direction toward the highway and Little Bridge on the other side of Roanoke Sound. Didn't have any business doing it, I knew, but it was as if I couldn't help myself. Wanted to be where the action was.

As I crested the bridge over the sound, the sun in my face and sparkling off the water like hundreds of diamonds, I could see activity on the left beyond the end of the bridge. Several police cars and the rescue squad were still there. An officer remained, now standing on the side of the road, to keep traffic moving. I put on my blinker to signal I wanted to park on the right. The officer tried to motion me forward, but I turned into the parking area on the right, despite his glare and angry waving of an arm. Lowering my window, I yelled to him that I needed to speak to Agent Twiddy. The officer didn't seem happy but I parked and smiled at him as I got out of my car.

As I waited on the edge of the road for a break in the traffic, the officer began to tolerate me. As always, there was wind there on the causeway and I zipped up my windbreaker. The sun helped dispel the chill of the breeze. The sun's warmth felt good on my shoulders and the side of my face. I could see Balls peering into the cab of the Nissan. I knew the dead man was still inside. Two EMTs stood waiting for Balls and Dr. Willis to give the word so they could remove the body. Then it came over me with a damp feeling of depression. It wasn't just a body; it was the lifeless remains of the frightened young man, the one with the tattoo on his neck, who sat in the booth behind us at breakfast, the young man who trembled with fear, knowing he had been made as an informant, and sensed terrifyingly that his time was limited. And it surely was. It ended no more than three or four minutes after he left the restaurant.

I crossed the road and got closer to Balls and Dr. Willis. One of the officers held his hand up, palm toward me to keep me from approaching. I stopped, but Balls saw the officer and mouthed an "okay" and the officer stepped back and dropped his hand.

Balls spoke softly to me. "This is the man I said I might want you to meet with."

"Yes, I figured." I tried not to look at the dead young man, but I couldn't help it. Dr. Willis had moved him to the right so he could see the other gunshot wounds. There was a lot of blood, and I turned back to Balls. "Any leads at all?"

Balls shook his head. "We're gonna get 'em though . . . Somehow," he added. But it didn't sound convincing.

I nodded, although I knew as well as Balls, that the assailants, the hit men, were too slick and their attack too well planned, to be caught easily. They would have to somehow make a mistake, do something stupid, or Balls and other lawmen would have to get very lucky.

Now that Balls' informant had been killed, and probably by the same ones who murdered Tom Applewaite and strung him up on channel marker number six, we had to wonder what would happen next, and I think I knew. "Willie Boy Applewaite?" I said.

Balls seemed distracted, like it took a moment for my

words to reach him. "Yeah," he mumbled. "I've got to get him, take him into protective custody whether he wants it or not." Then he became more animated and he said to Dr. Willis, "I'm through if you want them to take the body away."

"Yes," Dr. Willis sighed. "They can take him." He shook his head. "Pretty obvious what caused his death, but there'll have to be the official autopsy anyway over in Greenville."

Back to Balls again, I said, "So where is Willie Boy? Anyone know?"

Balls shook his head, puffed air out of one side of his mouth. Without speaking to me, pulled out his cell phone and punched in a number on speed dial. He held the phone close to his ear, turning his back from the highway where traffic was beginning to pick up as the officer waved vehicles through. Into his cell, Balls said, "Odell? Yeah, we need to secure Willie Boy Applewaite. We don't want anything to happen to him . . . yeah, yeah, I know he doesn't want to be with us. Doesn't make any difference. I want him in custody if necessary. We can come up with something to hold him on." Balls listened a moment. "If you can go down to Wanchese to get him that would be great. If not, send someone, but best if you do." Ball listened, as Deputy Wright said something him. "Yeah, I guess we might as well lift those roadblocks. They don't know what to be looking for anyway, not at this stage. Might have done some good if . . . well, never mind. Lift 'em."

Balls put his phone on his belt, twisted his mouth as if he were going to spit. He pulled that big handkerchief from his back pocket and wiped his face. He wasn't sweating, not with the breeze coming off the causeway, but he wiped his face anyway, as if trying to refresh himself.

To me he said, "This hasn't turned out to be a very good day, has it?"

A sad expression lined Balls' face. His big shoulders

sagged as if he had suddenly become tired. He cast his eyes to the ground, and then toward the EMTs loading the body of the young man into the ambulance, now serving as a hearse. He spoke softly, but I could hear him plainly: "Maybe there was something I could have done to keep Leroy safe. Not get him killed." But then the sadness was gone and I could see the anger rising in his eyes, in the set of his jaw.

"You can't take the blame for it," I said. "He knew the risks when he agreed to it."

Balls made a face like he tasted bile; he spit, his fists clenched at his side. "Life can sure be a bitch sometimes, can't it?"

"Tell me about it," I said.

Chief Deputy Odell Wright couldn't find Willie Boy Applewaite. Nor could any of the other deputies. Not in Wanchese or any of the other places they searched. It didn't really surprise me. I knew Willie Boy had his own agenda, and being found and taken into protective custody was not what he wanted. I knew, the same as Balls knew, that Willie Boy was off somewhere preparing to play Lone Ranger. That was a dangerous and deadly game to be playing with the characters that were involved. They were killers, and eliminating any sort of opposition to their lucrative drug business was paramount to them. I'd seen the type before. The lives of others had no meaning for them. They didn't care what they did, felt no remorse, as long as they kept their enterprise rolling.

Driving up to my little house in Kill Devil Hills, I burned with waves of anger over what was going on—the killings and the evil presence that appeared to be running lose, with authorities powerless to stop it. It was not my duty to intervene, or my right to do so, but I couldn't help it: I wanted to get in there and stop the sons of bitches responsible. I had known Tom Applewaite, if only slightly, and I had met his brother Willie Boy, whom I knew was in danger; and I had been in close proximity to terrified Leroy just minutes before he was gunned down. Maybe it's a flaw of mine, developed from long years as a crime writer, but I was infused inexorably with a determination to expose and put away the person or persons responsible for these killings.

I parked under the carport at my house, cut the engine. It was only midmorning but I felt bone tired and depleted.

Trudging up the outside stairs, I entered the kitchen and realized that in my hurry to meet Balls for breakfast, I'd left the coffeemaker on but it had turned itself off automatically after an hour or so. Just the same, there was the bitter smell of scorched coffee. I dumped the coffee grounds and put the cooled pot in the sink with water and detergent, let it soak.

Janey chirped at my presence and bobbed her head. "Okay, Janey," I said, "I'm glad to see you, too." And actually I was; her antics and noises always made me feel better.

I picked up my bass fiddle that lay as it usually did on its side in the middle of the living room. I had a stand for it over in one corner but rarely used it. Instead, you had to step over the neck of it as you moved around the living room. Oh, well, it was my house. I started to play a couple of jazz riffs. But I couldn't get into it, and I laid the bass down, and went to the sliding glass doors and stared out at the scrubby pine tree at the end of the deck. The more majestic live oak spread its low hanging branches over on the right, dominating the vacant lot. It was a nice, pleasant view, but I couldn't help thinking about what was going on. I tried to channel my mind to something else. So I decided to call Elly. Hearing her voice would help.

She answered at the Register of Deeds office on the first ring.

"Harrison," I said. She is virtually the only one who uses my first name. To everyone else I'm Weav or Weaver.

"I've been wondering where you were. I heard about the

. . . the shooting this morning on the causeway."

"Yes, that was bad."

"Not just bad. It was horrible. Are we living in some sort of war zone?"

"Seems that way today."

"You okay? You sound . . . I don't know. Tired? Depressed?" A trace of her "hoigh toide" accent came across faintly.

"I guess it just seems like the end of a long day . . . and it's still morning."

"You were out with Agent Twiddy . . . and all that?"

"Yes, but I'd just as soon not talk about it."

She paused. "I understand."

I wanted to change the subject. "How about tonight?"

I think she moved away from her coworkers, and then she spoke more softly. "I start at the Christmas Shop in the morning. So I thought I'd stay home tonight with Martin."

Then I remembered. "Oh, I did see one of the miniature golf places operating. I guess the mild weather, weekend coming up, they decided to be open. I can take Martin there in the morning."

"You sure you don't mind? He'd love it."

"Suppose I come to your house just before you leave for the Christmas Shop. Pick up Martin and head on out."

"Wonderful, Harrison. That's awfully nice of you."

"Maybe when we finish, and get some refreshments, we can swing by the Christmas Shop, let him see his mama at work there."

"I don't think Mr. Greene would mind."

"We won't stay, or disrupt anything." We chatted just a couple of more minutes, and then I said, "I guess I'd better fix some lunch."

"Another one of your ham sandwiches?" She laughed softly.

"Okay, smart-aleck, I want you to know that I've decided I'm going to get more creative in my cooking. I even bought a copy of Julia Child's *Mastering the Art of French Cooking.*"

"Inspired after our trip to Paris this spring?"

"Yes, maybe. Figured it was time to forsake those ham sandwiches. When I master some of the art of French cooking, I'll have you over for dinner . . . and maybe some delightful dessert afterward."

There was that soft laugh again. "That would be wonderful . . . and the dessert, too." I heard one of her coworkers say something in the background. "I'd better go now, Harrison. Talk with you later?"

We disconnected and I realized I was smiling a bit. So nice to have something like a normal conversation, not one laced with talk about murder and mayhem. But then, just like that, I realized I needed to call my editor and fill her in on what was happening down here in Magnoliaville.

I got through to Rose Mantelli right away. Immediately she said, "Saw something on the wires about a body strung up on a buoy or one of those maritime things. Wondered when in the hell you were going to call me about that. I don't run a quarterly, you know."

"Good to talk with you, too, Rose," I said.

She cackled and said, "Sounds like the beginning of a good one."

"I knew the fellow, the victim, slightly," I said.

"Sorry. But you know, the presses keep running, as the Brits would say."

With a suppressed chuckle in my voice, I said, "How do you know anything about what the Brits would say, Rose. You've never been beyond Thirty-Fourth Street in New York."

She liked the banter. "I'll have you know that several times I've watched PBS and they're forever talking British. I've picked up on it."

A moment later we got serious again. "I'm afraid that one slaying was just the beginning." And then I filled her in on the killing this morning and about the missing brother, Willie Boy.

"Is that really his name? Billy Bob Willie Boy, or whatever?"

"Willie Boy Applewaite," I said.

"Jesus, you live in a different world."

I said, "I believe this whole thing may unravel into a great deal more than just a couple of killings. It's sort of a miniature drug cartel, with a number of people involved. A long way from being solved at the moment but . . ."

Her excitement came across. "You may have another book here, Weaver."

"Right now it seems more personal than just a book. Too close to it to get any perspective."

She was quiet. Unusual for Rose. "Be careful, Weaver. I know how involved you get." Then the Brooklynite Rose came back: "Don't want to lose you. You're one of my best writers."

"I thought I was *the* best."

"Can always get you with that, can't I?" and her laughter became her usual mixture of cackle and cigarette-induced coughing.

After we hung up, I did make another one of my ham sandwiches. But I browsed through the Julia Child book as I ate in the sunshine on the deck, and I vowed I would become more creative in my cooking and meal preparations. Living alone was no excuse for not doing so.

Chapter Ten

Saturday morning I waked at six-thirty, started the coffee going and scurried in to take a quick shower. I must confess that my emotions were mixed concerning taking Martin to play miniature golf. It was not so much that I didn't want to take him; I guess I wondered how he would take to me without his mother with us. Wasn't sure he would be all that happy. Well, going to have to find out. Heck, maybe I was a tad nervous about it. Like a first date. I stepped out on the deck, greeting the early morning sunshine, coffee cup in hand. I kept telling myself, no big deal. Go with the flow, that sort of crap.

I went back inside and Janey bounced up and down a bit and said "Shit" just as plain as day.

Grinning at her, I came back with "Bitch."

She repeated it.

Now that we had run through her complete vocabulary, she was content with chirping and making other ordinary parakeet noises.

By shortly after eight, I was on my way to Manteo and Elly's house. We were blessed with another gorgeous mild December day and I was determined to concentrate on normal, everyday activities, try not to think about investigations and all of the unsavory stuff that I knew bubbled just below the surface.

I pulled into Elly's gravel driveway less than thirty minutes later. She did not come out on the front porch. I knew she'd be hurrying to get ready to go to her first day at work at the Christmas Shop. She'd be happily excited about it, too.

Stepping on the front porch, I tapped lightly at the door. From inside, Elly called for me to come in.

Martin was dressed and sat rather stiffly on one of the living room chairs. He eyed me seriously. He may have nodded.

"Be right out," Elly said. Then, her voice louder: "Martin, get your jacket."

"I've got it," he said, not taking his eyes off me. His little brown jacket was folded neatly in his lap.

Elly came into the living room, her face a little flushed with excitement. She had a touch of lipstick and her dark hair was pulled back and affixed with a clip of some kind. She wore beige tailored slacks and a blue-gray long-sleeve blouse, a tiny gold chain around her neck. She gave me a quick peck on the cheek. She smelled good, as always, like fresh cotton and sunshine.

"You ready to go with Mr. Weaver, Martin?"

He didn't look all that happy.

"Lauren?" Martin asked.

Elly turned to me. "Oh, my goodness. I didn't mention this to you, Harrison. Sorry. But could you take Lauren with you, too?" She sounded flustered. "This came up this morning, and . . ."

"No problem at all," I said.

We heard Lauren and her mother come to the front door.

Under her breath, Elly said again, "I'm sorry, Harrison. I should have . . ." Then speaking up, she said, "Come on in, Mary and Lauren."

Elly introduced Lauren's mother, Mary, to me. The mother was short, her face round, like Lauren's, dressed in jeans and a light denim jacket. No makeup.

I said I would bring both of them back around noon or

so. We might get something to eat first. Both Elly and Mary made a big deal out of my taking the children to play miniature golf.

Lauren looked up at me and said, "We going to Sweet Toads?"

"It's Sweet Frogs," Martin said, "not Toads." He referred to a festive frozen yogurt establishment that had a myriad of toppings for the yogurt.

"Well, maybe after Putt-Putt," I said. "Probably not open yet. Tell you what, we'll stop at Dunkin' Donuts instead. How about that?"

"I want one of the chocolate ones with sprinkles on top of it," Lauren said.

"Me, too," Martin said, and for the first time he smiled.

Elly excused herself, saying she had to get something in the back. Mary stood about a little awkwardly, then said she was glad to have met me, finally, and that Elly had talked about me quite a bit, and she said how nice it was of me to be doing this, and still talking she opened the front door and called back to Elly that she'd see her later. Then, even louder, she called, "You've got a good one here, Elly. Hang on to him." She grinned and headed next door.

It was now close to nine. Elly came to the living room, a light jacket over her right arm. She glanced at the newspaper lying on the sofa opened to the crossword. I could see her hesitate. "No," she said more to herself. "I won't take it."

Mrs. Pedersen stuck her head into the living room, smiled at me and shook her head. "Lots of activity, hustle and bustle around here this Saturday morning." Then to me, her smile broadening, "And good luck to you this morning as you go on this adventure." She nodded at the two children.

With Martin buckled in the passenger seat and Lauren buckled behind him (despite her protest that she sit in the front seat also), we followed Elly into Manteo and waved at her as she turned left into the parking lot of the Island Gallery and Christmas Shop. She waved one hand and tapped her horn lightly once.

"We'll go back there to see Mama after Putt-Putt?" Martin said.

"Yes," I said. "Absolutely."

"But not until after Sweet Toads," Lauren intoned from the backseat.

"Sweet Frogs," Martin corrected, staring straight ahead. "And we're not going there. We're going to Ducking Donuts."

"It's Dunkin' Donuts, smarty," Lauren said. "Not ducks."

We drove past one of the miniature golf places on the Bypass that was closed. "We'll go up farther," I said. "There's one open up ahead. But first Dunkin' Donuts because the golf place is probably not even open yet. Not until about ten."

"I have to be in bed before ten," Lauren said quietly.

"I mean ten in the morning, not night," I said.

Martin shook his head and started to say something to Lauren, but then apparently checked himself and kept his mouth shut.

We turned left off the Bypass into the Dunkin' Donut parking. They wanted to rush in and I watched for other cars as I let them get unbuckled and out. They went straight to the counter, ready to order. The attractive young woman behind the counter looked down at them with a smile. Martin and Lauren both pointed at the same time. "The chocolate ones with the sprinkle stuff on top," they said in almost perfect unison.

"For here or to go?" the young woman asked. She had a lilt to her speech, an accent from one of the Eastern European countries, maybe part of the former Soviet Union. There was a work program that permitted a number of them to come here to work during the summer, and some of them managed to stay on.

"Oh, we're going to eat them now," Martin said.

"We've had breakfast," Lauren added demurely.

I ordered a sugared donut and small black coffee and got two hot chocolates for them. I figured they'd be on something of a sugar high, but maybe the miniature golf would take care of it. They wanted to sit at the high round table, and I had to help them up onto the wooden stools with the curved backs.

Before we left, they split one more donut. This one a plain glazed one. They had to wait for the hot chocolate to cool enough to drink. Other patrons came in and left, and we still sat there, the number of used paper napkins beginning to build up.

During a lull, the young woman looked at us and smiled. She came from behind the counter to clear off a table. "They yours?" she asked.

"No, I'm just the babysitter today."

"We're going to play Putt-Putt," Martin said.

"I'll probably win," Lauren added.

"Will not."

The young woman laughed.

"Where you from? Originally?" I asked.

She smiled again, "Moldova. Small country. You know where it is?"

"Oh, yes," I said. "I've never been there but it's next to Romania and the Ukraine."

"A pretty country," she said, "but we're poor."

"Your English is good," I said.

"I study it hard in school," she said and she smiled and nodded and hurried back behind the counter.

Martin finished the last of his hot chocolate. I pointed to one of several napkins and he wiped his mouth. He said, "She's not from here, the Outer Banks?"

"Well, she is now," I said as we got up, clearing up paper napkins and wiping off the table a bit. I put something in the tip jar as we left and Martin and Lauren waved at the young woman from Moldova.

When we drove up the Bypass to the one opened miniature golf facility, they selected their clubs and then went through periods of indecision over which colored balls to play with. Once decided, we made our way to the first tee. Lauren went first. A mighty whack. Too much of one, but with a kick with one foot she got the ball back on the "fairway." Martin did a bit better, and I followed along. We didn't really keep score, although I pretended to do so. It was interesting to watch their intensity with which they played. And they didn't fuss with each other too much. Another couple with two young children started in behind us. I was concerned on a couple of holes as Lauren and Martin hit multiple times trying to make their putts, that we might have to let the other people play through. But our game picked up, and at the eighteenth hole Lauren was disappointed that the ball disappeared back into the shop. Game over.

I had really enjoyed the whole thing. It was warm enough that I was beginning to sweat. Martin had tied his jacket around his waist so that it looked from the rear as though he were wearing a type of sarong.

Then we made our way down to Sweet Frogs. I was surprised they were open. Frozen yogurt with a myriad of toppings. More sugar. I would be taking them home later where they could be nursed back to good health in a day or so. When we got back in the car, after individual trips to the restroom, Martin still wanted to sit up front. "I have to help him drive," he told Lauren.

"You're not helping at all," Lauren said.

"I have to tell him where the Christmas Shop is so we can go see Mama."

"He knows where the Christmas Shop is, silly."

I got them buckled up and quieted down and we headed back to Manteo.

Pulling into the Christmas Shop parking lot, I found a place near the front. We prepared to go in and I told them both to stay close to me and not wander off.

"Oh, I love this place," Lauren said. "Smells good, too. Always like Christmas."

And it did smell like Christmas, and all year long. Enticing fragrances wafted, not overwhelming but there to remind you. Soft Christmas music played from hidden speakers.

"I know all about this place," Martin said, the trace of a swagger in his walk. "My Mama works here part-time and just about runs the place."

"She just started," Lauren said.

"Doesn't matter."

"Okay, you two," I said. "Be nice and behave yourselves. We'll only go in and speak to Martin's mother . . . and stay out of the way of everyone."

Inside, after as quick a look at the ornaments to the left as I could manage with the two of them, we headed straight back and then to the right to the jewelry room. Tina, with her usual big and engaging smile, waited on an elderly woman, and Elly stood behind the adjoining counter showing jewelry to a man who looked vaguely familiar. He stood peering at items in the glass case. Elly spotted us and brightened immediately. Martin started to go over to her but I held on to his hand and he got the message. Lauren was fascinated by a rack of earrings.

Elly said, "Come on over. Want you to meet someone." Then to the man she said, "It's my son, Martin, and his friend Lauren . . ." She gazed at me, her eyes bright, ". . . and my friend Harrison Weaver." She added, "They've been playing Putt-Putt."

"I won," Martin announced.

"You did not," Lauren said. "And we went to Sweet Toads and got donuts, too, with those sprinkle things."

"And hot chocolate," Martin said.

We went close to the counter. I held on to Martin's hand. With a grin, I said, "They'll be healthy again in a day or two." I put out my hand to the man standing there. "I'm

Harrison Weaver," I said.

"Gregory Loudermilk," he said, shaking my hand with a reasonably firm grip. He appeared to be in his early thirties, about Elly's age. He was neatly dressed in a button-down shirt and slacks, a nice looking sweater, topped with a fashionable denim sport coat. His loafers were polished. His medium blond hair was sharply parted and brushed back along the sides. I realized I'd seen him around the courthouse. An attorney, I assumed. He said, "Getting a Christmas present . . . I hope." He smiled again.

I thought about asking, "For your wife?" But I nodded instead.

Elly spoke up. "Gregory is looking for something suitable for his mother. Isn't that sweet?"

I nodded again and said something mundane and a little foolish like, "Well, there's plenty to choose from here."

"Sure is," he said, "and that's part of the problem."

I kept a firm grip on Martin's hand. He wanted to get around the counter to his mother. "I'd better get them on out of here," I said. "Take them home—to your house."

"It was awfully nice for you to take them to play Putt-Putt," Elly said. She gave a light chuckle, "And to load them up with sugar."

"I want to stay here awhile," Lauren said, a bit of a pout on her face.

"We'll look at some of the ornaments up front," I said. "Martin, tell your mother bye." To Gregory Loudermilk I said, "Didn't mean to interrupt your shopping, and decision-making."

"No problem at all," he said, flashing perfect teeth.

I already didn't like him. He was too neat, too well groomed, and . . . well . . . perfect. He made me feel somewhat scruffy. With my one free hand I patted down the cowlick at the back of my head, and tried to smooth down the front of my windbreaker. Maybe the stirrings of a bit of green-eyed envy as Elly turned her attention back to Gregory

Loudermilk.

As we were leaving the jewelry room, Tina had finished with her customer and she came out into the hall to say hello. "I'm so glad Elly is here to help me out. She's wonderful."

We were standing there grinning and chatting when Christmas Shop owner Edward Greene came zipping by in the hallway sitting astride the motorized electric four-wheel scooter he uses. The scooter looks like a miniature one-person topless golf cart. He saw us and stopped quickly.

He has an elfish smile that captivates. I shook his hand. Always pleased to see him, speak to him, hear one of the many stories he can tell. Catch up on the latest gossip from town.

He launched right into his latest theories about the killing of Tom Applewaite and the young man on the causeway. "All of it drug-related," he pronounced.

I shrugged. "Probably so."

"Have you heard about the press conference set for Monday?" he said, his brown eyes sparkling. "It will be almost a town meeting, with everyone there. Including the mayor, and Rick Schweikert, Sheriff Albright . . . the works."

I was startled. "No. When did this get announced?"

"I am not sure it's even officially announced yet. It will be though. Some of the people in the county, and reporters, too, of course, have been requesting it."

His voice became softer, conspiratorial, and he leaned forward toward me in his scooter. "There's talk about getting rid of Sheriff Albright. That he's not tough enough on crime."

With a frown concerning any such talk, I said, "Albright's a good man."

"Too good, some people are saying." He stared up at me, his eyes serious.

"When and where is this press conference or town meeting supposed to be?"

"Eleven o'clock Monday at the courthouse. It will be in the big room upstairs."

While I talked with Edward Greene, Tina had kept the children corralled in the hallway. Two women shoppers strolled toward us and Mr. Greene said, "I better get out of the way. Let our customers have the space." He twisted the handle on his scooter chair and away he went.

I smiled briefly at the two shoppers as they glanced at paintings on the wall, and then they moved into the jewelry room, with Tina handing off the children to me and following the women. I realized I now had a frown on my face. "Come on, children," I said, and secured their hands to mine.

Eugene Albright had been sheriff for at least twelve years. He had been a deputy under the late Sheriff Claxton. He was a big bear of a man with a kindly somewhat fleshy face. I'd always felt he would much rather try to keep youngsters out of trouble than arresting any of them. I thought about how he had tried to counsel the Applewaite brothers.

Elly excused herself from Gregory Loudermilk, turning him over temporarily to Tina, and she stepped out into the hall as I started to leave. I smiled at her and said, "Guess I'd better deliver these two sugar-laden plums back to your house."

She brought Martin's hand up in hers and touched my arm. "It was so very, very nice of you to take them out this morning. That was special."

"We had fun."

"I think I won," Martin said.

"No you didn't. It was a tie," Lauren countered.

Elly cast her eyes toward the ceiling. "Good luck," she said to me. She bent down and gave Martin a kiss on the top of his head. "Be good and I'll see you at suppertime." She patted Lauren's head lightly. "You children be sure to thank Mr. Weaver."

We left and I drove them westward to Elly's home and delivered them to Mrs. Pedersen. While I stood on the porch speaking with her, Lauren's mother came over, dressed as she had been earlier, and thanked me profusely for taking Lauren. "We had fun," I said again, and started backing away from the porch.

At Mrs. Pedersen and Lauren's mother's urging, both of the children mumbled thank-you.

"They'd both better get regular food for the rest of the day," I said with a laugh, and headed for my car.

As I drove away, I knew I needed to talk with Balls, get his take on the press conference that Mr. Greene said would take place Monday. Make sure it was going to happen. Balls would be there, if in fact there was going to be such an event. I took a left onto Budleigh Street when I got into Manteo and pulled into a space near the courthouse. I punched in Balls' cell number on my phone. After three rings I didn't think he would answer, and then his voice, "I'm on the road."

"You know about a press conference Monday?"

"Yeah." He didn't sound happy about it.

"See you there?"

"Sure."

"Understand some folks may not be happy with the good sheriff."

He didn't respond immediately, and then he said, "Not actually *some*, as in a number of people, but more like one or two people with their own agenda."

I wanted to find out more. But Balls said, "I'm going home. Got a wife, you know."

"See you Monday," I said, but he had already disconnected.

I hoped that things would remain quiet the rest of the weekend. We'd certainly had enough happenings for a while.

On Sunday, I drove the short distance up to Henry's for a late breakfast. At the cash register and high counter, I spoke to Linda. She and her husband own the restaurant, a favorite for many of the locals.

From Cory, the young redheaded waitress who came immediately to my booth, I ordered the special three-egg omelet with American cheese and ham, a tall glass of tomato juice with ice, buttered toast. Before she left I asked how her cousin Michelle's son was doing. Michelle had worked at another restaurant and also part-time at one of the doctor's office. Her son, about Martin's age, had developed severe kidney problems early on, and Michelle had been frantically taking him back and forth for medical treatment up to a highly regarded facility in Virginia Beach.

Cory brightened and said, "Oh, he's doing much better. I saw Michelle yesterday." She nodded enthusiastically. "I think he's started doing real good."

In just a few minutes Cory delivered my breakfast. She asked if I didn't want coffee. I declined, saying I had just about coffee-ed out this morning. Actually, I'm rather picky about my coffee, and I'd fixed a strong pot of French roast before I ventured out that morning.

After I ate, I decided to ride down to the beach access at Kill Devil Hills bathhouse to pay my respects to the ocean. If the NOAA weather report was accurate, and it usually was, this unseasonably mild weather was about to change by this afternoon. I wanted to take advantage of it before that happened. A low front was off the ocean and was expected to bring in a chilling and misty northeast wind, accompanied by a drop in temperature of about thirty degrees.

Four vehicles were parked in the lot at the Kill Devil Hills bathhouse. It was a few minutes past eleven. I strolled slowly up the wooden walkway to the beach overlook, paused there and listened to the ocean and watched the waves brushing against the beach, receding, and doing it endlessly. I looked out to the horizon and the sharp line between the end of the world and the sky.

While I stood there, I began to sense a change in the weather. Nothing I could see yet. But I could feel something.

Maybe it was a change in the atmospheric pressure that the body could sense without being able to define it.

Then I saw it. The front, coming in from the northeast. Almost as if by magic, a gray mass of clouds stretching from the surface of the ocean to high in the sky was moving in. A wall of low pressure, misty, cold rain. It was still in the far distance, but it was coming. Before it got much closer, the temperature began to drop. I watched for a few more minutes, turned and went back to my car just as the front descended, obliterating the sun and the last vestiges of the mild weather. A mist formed on my windshield before I left the parking lot. I had to bump the wipers on intermittently.

I headed home. On a day like today, with Elly at work at the Christmas Shop, with rather chilly and misty rain, it was a good day to stay home. When I got home, I sat in the living room and looked out at the overcast sky that dripped down mist and occasional light rain. I thought about the Willie Nelson song with the opening line: *This Looks Like a December Day*. Most appropriate. For it certainly did look like a December day.

Janey eyed me and wondered why I sat so still. She liked activity, unless she was napping. Later I ate a light snack of fruit and cheese and decided I would take a nap.

It had turned out to be a peaceful Sunday, with the entire weekend relaxing and pleasant.

But early Monday morning it was a different story.

Chapter Eleven

Not even fully light Monday morning when my phone rang. I reached over to the nightstand beside my bed for the receiver.

It was Balls.

"Been two more," he said.

I could hear road noise and knew he was talking on his hands-free device while he drove.

"Where?"

"Up from you. The Marketplace, Southern Shores. Victims, two guys sitting in their car."

"Jeeze."

"I'm on my way. Twenty minutes out." Phone clicked off.

I threw on some clothes. Thought about a cup of coffee but time ruled against it. I uncovered Janey's cage while staring out the front windows at the weather. Rain had more or less stopped but it was still overcast and the top of my pine tree struggled with the wind coming from the northeast. Probably low forties. I grabbed a heavier, water-repellent windbreaker, my Greek fisherman's cap, a pen and slim reporter's notebook, and I was out of there and on my way north toward The Marketplace shopping center at Mile Post 1. I thought about the press conference scheduled for eleven that morning. Well, there'd certainly be more to talk about but I doubted if a press conference was on Balls' list of things to do, not with two more bodies.

Making the first turn into the shopping center off Juniper, I looked for what would be plenty of activity and flashing lights. They were clearly visible. Cruisers clustered near two large trees at the far corner of the parking area, close to the Bypass and the main entrance to The Marketplace. I continued past Food Lion and CVS and pulled within a respectable distance of the group of officers and three police vehicles: two from Southern Shores, one Dare County. Two officers cordoned off the scene with yellow tape. I heard another siren and a Dare County ambulance wheeled into The Marketplace, came to a stop within inches of the yellow tape.

I got out of my Subaru, stood there for a moment, watching, figuring how close I could get. Then out of the corner of my eye I saw Balls speeding in at the driveway entrance at the north end. No siren but his flasher light pulsated atop his Thunderbird. He nudged the yellow tape with the nose of his car. I had moved quickly over to stand near him as he got out and lifted the tape and went under it. I followed right behind him as if I had a right to be there. None of the officers tried to stop me. Balls was so intent on getting to the scene that he completely ignored me. But he had to be aware I was tagging along, dogging him.

He nodded at young Dare County Deputy Dorsey, who stood near the driver's door of the black BMW sedan. His usually ruddy complexion now somewhat ashen. Balls went to the driver's window, which was fully open, and peered in. I hung back only slightly. The driver, dressed in a black suit, slumped toward the steering wheel, a neat bullet hole in his head just above his jaw line. Another man, dressed about the same way, leaned toward the passenger door, his right arm outstretched in death as if he reached for the handle, too late. He had a great deal of blood on his upper body. Both men appeared to be in their forties.

A young Southern Shores officer approached Balls and identified himself as the one who, on routine patrol that morning, had checked out the car, parked there overnight, and discovered the bodies inside. At first he thought they were sleeping. Balls listened to him but kept sweeping the scene with his gaze.

"Not ID'd yet," Balls mumbled, referring to the victims. "Run the tags?"

"Yes sir. It's a rental. Probably Norfolk airport."

Balls nodded.

I had gotten too close and Balls gave me a quick frown and I stepped back with Deputy Dorsey.

Whispering to me, Dorsey said, "I'll betcha these are the two hit men that did the shooting on the causeway. They're not from here. Least they don't look local."

I watched as Balls carefully opened the driver's door, using his ever-present handkerchief to do the job. He felt around the left hip of the driver, apparently looking for a wallet with identification. Nothing there.

Deputy Dorsey was beginning to warm to speculation. "Maybe these are the two guys that did that to Tom Applewaite, strung him up and all." His voice got more animated. "And his brother, Willie Boy. You know we haven't found him yet." He narrowed his eyes. "I just wonder if maybe Willie Boy . . ." He let his voice trail off.

I started to say something, but instead gave a noncommittal shrug. I thought about the fact that the driver's window was down, not shattered with bullets.

Leaning away from Dorsey, I watched as the trunk of the BMW popped open and Balls and an officer bent forward to inspect the contents. They didn't touch anything. Balls gave an affirmative nod of his head, as if whatever was in the trunk confirmed his thinking. I took two steps toward the BMW. I could see inside the trunk. Laid out on oiled towels were at least two automatic weapons. Maybe a couple of handguns, also. I don't know what kind, but they looked mean and lethal, and I'm sure they were. Balls pushed the lid of the trunk down gently, again using his handkerchief.

Then Balls looped around to the passenger side of the car, peered in the window but didn't open the door. I think he figured the body of the man would fall out if he did.

A North Carolina Highway Patrol car arrived, and so did another police car, this one from Kitty Hawk. Curious bystanders were beginning to arrive. Officers kept them at a distance. I saw Bonnie from Bonnie's Bagels eyeing the scene from the sidewalk in front of her business, a hundred yards away.

I checked the time. It was only eight o'clock. The two medics from the ambulance stood off to the side. Then another volunteer medical until, this one from Southern Shores, pulled into the area. The EMTs from the two units gathered together and talked, glancing toward the BMW and awaiting instructions as to what to do next. One of the EMTs had come to the BMW earlier, and clearly saw there was nothing they could do as far as resuscitation was concerned. Their vehicles would serve as hearses, if anything.

Balls was on his cell phone. He clicked off. To the deputy with him, he said, "They'll be here shortly. Won't move anything until the lab guys arrive."

He spoke about the SBI lab technicians, probably the ones in Elizabeth City. Maybe they were already on their way. Balls wanted fingerprints, if possible from the vehicle, and certainly from the victims. I sensed that there was no identification on the bodies. I expected they were careful about that. Who were these guys? I had my opinion, and I wanted to check it with Balls when I could manage to get close enough to him. Right now might be a good time, since there was something of a waiting game going on until the lab technicians arrived.

Balls checked his watch. Gave a big sigh, looked at the vehicle, and strode to the side a few steps. He said something to one of the officers, who in turn spoke to the others, and everyone stood around, waiting. The Highway Patrol officer came up to Balls and conversed quietly. Balls shook his head and the officer appeared ready to leave.

I was a little surprised none of the officers had questioned what I was doing at the scene, but I supposed it was because I came up in the beginning and entered under the yellow tape at the same time Balls did. Too, most of the officers knew me, or knew who I was, and that I was a friend of Balls.

I inched over close to Balls, who stood a bit apart at the moment from the others.

"The hit men?" I said.

He looked at me, and beyond, as if running something through his mind. Then he came back to me and said, "Probably."

I shook my head. "Not Willie Boy."

He sighed again. "Nope."

I said, "Window down. They weren't expecting trouble. Caught by surprise."

He managed half a smile from one corner of his mouth. "You're getting pretty good at this sort of thing. Sticking around with me."

Then he said, "Question is, though, why were they done in? And by who?"

"Whom," I said. "By whom."

"Huh?" Then, "Screw you." But Balls almost managed a grin.

He pondered something, hands thrust deep in his pockets. "Someone doesn't want any loose ends left around—even guys who may have been hired specifically to do a job." He squinted his eyes in thought, as if he was beginning to hit on something. "Possible it was done by the very guy who hired them . . . if these are actually the pros who've done the other things." He nodded more to himself. "And I believe they are."

Balls gave a quick, but penetrating look at my face.

"I've been thinking that you being with me there at the Dunes when Leroy came in might've put you in some danger, too. No telling what these guys, or someone else, might think you know. Want you eliminated."

"Really a comforting thought, Balls." I shook my head. But what about you?"

He made a snorting noise. "They'd know better'n mess with an SBI agent." He gave a quick grin, and was back to the here and now.

He straightened his shoulders and took purposeful steps back close to the BMW. To one of the officers he said, "When the lab guys run prints on these two I'll betcha we get hits. They're in the system, I just know it."

With two or three quick steps, Balls came back to me. "That press conference. You're going?" It was as if he'd just remembered it.

"Plan to," I said.

"Take notes and fill me in later." He shook his head. "They'll have plenty to talk about now. That's for sure."

And no sooner had he said that than we saw two additional vehicles speed up, lights flashing atop one of them, and the other—a plain black Ford—right behind it. They pulled up close.

"Uh-oh," Balls muttered. "We just got more official."

The Dare County cruiser was driven by Chief Deputy Odell Wright. Sheriff Albright, in full uniform with a tie neatly knotted, but slightly askew, sat solemnly beside him, his big bulk somehow seeming to dwarf the front seat. Wright cut the flashing light and swept out of the cruiser. Albright emerged stiffly, stood beside the vehicle, viewing the scene and shaking his large head sadly. Balls shook hands with both men and spoke quietly to the sheriff. All three men were about the same height, five-eleven or so, and made quite an impressive trio as they walked over to the BMW to inspect the scene.

Quickly joining them, and certainly not to be left out,

was DA Rick Schweikert, who was driving the black Ford. As usual, he was dressed in a stiffly starched white shirt and tie, his blondish hair cut short, almost a buzz cut. And as usual, he glared at me as he passed by to join the three others. No love lost on either side—him or me.

As if being drawn by a magnet, here came Linda Shackleford, a reporter-photographer for *The Coastland Times*, and a friend of mine and long-time friend of Elly's. Right behind her the bulky TV remote truck from one of the Norfolk stations arrived from the north and got as close as officers would permit. Another reporter, a woman who was a correspondent for *The Virginian-Pilot*, stood back several yards from the yellow tape, surveying the scene with a look of apprehension, as if she didn't want to get too close to seeing something that would give her bad dreams.

The fact that they were all here didn't surprise me. They all had police scanner radios, and I was sure I would see them, and probably others, in a couple of hours at the press conference.

Linda Shackleford snapped a couple of pictures of the four men gathered at the side of the victims' car. An officer appeared to debate with himself as to whether to try to stop her but then obviously decided there was nothing he could do, or should do. She motioned to me and I came over and spoke to her. I stayed on the inside of the yellow tape. Didn't want to lose my place. Linda knew the basics—two unidentified white males shot to death in their car while parked at The Marketplace shopping center. The shooting taking place sometime during the night and discovered early by a Southern Shores officer on patrol.

"Maybe we'll get more at the press conference," Linda said.

"Maybe," I said, "but kind of doubt it. Not much more than that known at this point."

Turning my attention to the quartet at the BMW, I saw Sheriff Albright checking his watch, and then saying something to Deputy Wright, who nodded in agreement. Albright spoke to Balls, who shook his head. I assumed he was telling Albright he would not be at the press conference, or town meeting, or whatever it turned out to be. Schweikert would be there, standing front and center.

With a grim expression and the weight of the world on his shoulders, Sheriff Albright moved toward his car, Deputy Wright beside him.

Schweikert said something else to Balls, who gave Schweikert a blank stare. Schweikert hesitated a moment, as if he wanted to make another comment, then he ducked his head a couple of times quickly, and caught up with Albright and Wright.

They left, as they had arrived, one car following the other.

I excused myself from Linda, and went to Balls. "I'll get with you after the dog and pony show is over."

"Can hardly wait," he said dispiritedly, staring at the two bodies in the BMW.

Chapter Twelve

I got to Manteo by ten-thirty and parked a half block from the courthouse on Sir Walter Raleigh Street. Checking the sky, I took off my cap and left it on the passenger seat. Time enough for an espresso, maybe a muffin, at the coffee shop upstairs across from the courthouse. Inside the coffee shop, I placed my order, and wolfed down a muffin. With a to-go coffee cup in my hand, I stepped out on the porch. Even though the northeast wind was still chilling and the sky was densely overcast, at least it wasn't raining. From my vantage point on the upstairs porch, I waved to Jamie Layton, owner of Downtown Books, as she stood for a moment in the doorway of her store. I finished my coffee and hurried to the courthouse. Wanted to make sure I got a seat close enough to see the people, hear the questions and responses, but not get in the way of the reporters on deadline.

There'd be several reporters—plus the interested townspeople, and I expected more of the latter than the former.

When I went upstairs at the courthouse, there were already several people present, including two of the county commissioners, Manteo Mayor Susan Blanchard, who had her jacket on and didn't appear prepared to remain for the meeting. A trio of people stood near the back talking. Two men and a woman. Her name was Patsy something; one of the men was Boyd Bruton from the Southern Shores area;

the other man I'd not seen before. Bruton is portly, with a face as round as his stomach, and in fact has played Santa Claus at many of the Christmas functions. I assumed he would do the same this year. His eyes were beady and didn't seem to fit the rest of his face, but maybe it was the fat of his face that made them appear small. Patsy talked animatedly to the man I'd not seen before. He was tall with a narrow face and he looked down at Patsy and nodded from time to time. I heard her say, "And two more this morning, or last night. Right there in Southern Shores."

I sat near the front but to one side so that I had a good view of the entire room. A podium was set up in front of the bench where a judge usually sat. The room was filling with people. Linda Shackleford took a seat at the front, and so did the reporter from *The Virginian-Pilot* I'd seen at The Marketplace. Two more reporters came in to sit up front. There was a TV reporter I'd seen on one of the channels. He spoke to a couple of the reporters, shook hands, and took a seat, after looking around at the growing audience.

Right at eleven o'clock, the door behind the podium opened and in came Sheriff Albright, Rick Schweikert, and Deputy Odell Wright. Mabel, the long-time employee in the sheriff's office, shuffled in behind them and took one of the four chairs behind the podium. She carried a note pad and a portable recorder. Sheriff Albright's tie had been straightened, but he appeared most uncomfortable. A small microphone angled forward on the podium, and an amplifier sat on the floor off to one side.

Sheriff Albright tried a smile as he surveyed the room, now almost completely filled, with a few people standing at the rear even though there were still seats available.

The TV reporter bounced up and placed a recorder on the podium, and another of the reporters did the same thing. Standing a few steps from the podium, Albright eyed the recorders as if they might be explosives of some kind. He took a step toward the podium, cleared his throat, and tapped uncertainly on the microphone. It was live. He cleared his throat again.

"Good morning," Albright said. "Thank all of you for coming." He held a piece of notepaper in his right hand, and he laid the paper on the podium, and smoothed the creases with his fingers. He moistened his lips with the tip of his tongue. "First of all," he said, glancing at his notepaper, "I'll have a brief statement, and then we'll take questions from the media. After that we'll open the floor for discussions from anyone who would like to speak." For the first time he took notice of the glass of water that was under the lip of the podium. He picked up the glass and took a quick sip.

"We're having this meeting, this press conference, this morning at the request of . . . of several people . . . and we want to bring you up to date on our investigation of . . . of the recent acts of violence. And as I'm sure most of you have heard, there were two victims found this morning up at the north end of the islands." He glanced down again at his notes and appeared to be reading. "Now this is an ongoing investigation, so there are things I can tell you, some things that I cannot for fear of jeopardizing the investigation." He looked up at the audience. "And there are some things that we just don't know . . . yet, anyway."

A soft murmur arose from one or two people near the rear.

Schweikert, standing ramrod straight on Albright's right, tilted his head toward the sheriff and may have made a small sound in his throat. Albright did a quick, short nod. "Before we start with the questions, Mr. Schweikert would like to make a brief statement."

The sheriff stepped aside and Schweikert took command of the podium. "We want everyone to know that we will not rest in our duties until the perpetrators of these heinous crimes, these brutal, outrageous acts have been prosecuted to the fullest extent . . ." He continued orating for a minute or so longer. I think he mentioned "heinous" and "perpetrators" a couple more times. From past exposure to him, I knew they were two of his favorite words.

Then he turned the podium back to Sheriff Albright, who appeared much more willing to stay in the background. But he took a breath and said, "We'll now take questions from the media."

First to his feet was the TV reporter, while his cameraman ran a shoulder-mounted video camera from the side. "Sheriff, with two more killings just this morning, would you say you've got a virtual crime wave or gang war of some kind going on here at the Outer Banks?"

Sheriff Albright, his head tilted to the side, worked his mouth as if he was ready to speak, but the TV reporter continued before Albright got out his first word.

"And the second part of the question, Sheriff, do you think all four of these killings—all within a week's time—are connected? Is there a pattern here?"

Albright stared at his notepaper, and then at the reporter. "As I said in the beginning, this is an ongoing investigation and we don't want to start off by jumping to conclusions and speculating on a lot of stuff . . . a lot of theories . . . we have no basis for . . . for speculating on."

Another reporter, one I hadn't seen before today, stood and identified himself as a correspondent for the AP. He said, "Can you reveal to us the identity of the two men who were found slain in their car this morning?"

"Officers, including the SBI, are working on getting their identities right now," Albright said. He took another sip of his water and cast his eyes questioningly toward Deputy Wright. Wright gave a short shake of his head. "But no, we don't have their identity yet."

Linda Shackleford squirmed a bit in her chair and I knew she was getting up her courage to ask a question. She took advantage of the moment the AP correspondent sat down to raise her hand as if in school. Sheriff Albright nodded at her. "Linda?"

"Sheriff, do you have any suspects, or people of interest, you are looking for?"

Schweikert stepped forward before the sheriff could respond. "Linda, we can't make comments about that. We don't want to give information that could in any way jeopardize our investigation and the eventual prosecution of the perpetrator, or perpetrators." He stepped back, obviously pleased with himself.

The sheriff nodded in agreement.

Of course I took issue privately with Schweikert's statement about "our investigation." He doesn't do investigations; he prosecutes after the investigation has been completed.

The TV reporter stood again. "So the only thing you can actually tell us at this stage is what we already know: that there have been four killings in the past week, but we have no suspects, no motives, and we don't know whether the killings are related in any way." He gave a dramatic shake to his head. "In short, sir, you're not able to tell us anything."

There was more murmuring from the audience.

Sheriff Albright glared at the reporter. His voice was firm: "That's absolutely correct. And we're not going to say anything until we actually know something, and know it is factual."

"Thank you," the TV reporter said, and gave a slight smile.

From the rear of the room, the diminutive woman I knew only as Patsy stood up. While she was tiny, her voice wasn't. She spoke loudly, a strident tone overriding: "Sheriff Albright, with all due respect, do you think you need to bring in more professionals, more experienced lawmen, to get to the bottom of all these killings? It's like we've got a war going on. We can't help but wonder how safe any of us are."

Another murmur of agreement arose from the audience of townspeople in the back.

Sheriff Albright leaned his forearms on the podium, his big head thrust forward. "Ma'am, we *do* have experienced lawmen on this investigation, and they are working diligently and professionally. At this very moment, an agent from the State Bureau of Investigation is at the scene up at Southern Shores. He is leading the investigation along with . . ." and he inclined his head toward Wright ". . . Dare County Chief Deputy Odell Wright."

Albright straightened his stance, his voice still firm: "As for safety of all of you, I don't think you have anything to worry about." He paused, choosing his words carefully. "Although we are still in the very preliminary stages of the investigation, as I have indicated, it does appear that all of the victims—well, they do not appear to be the average citizen on the street. Not random." He wrinkled his brow as if maybe in anger he had said too much.

The TV reporter jumped to his feet. "In other words, Sheriff, are you saying that in fact these killings may be related?"

Somewhat more quietly, Sheriff Albright said, "I really can't comment on that."

The TV guy again: "Can I take that as a 'Yes, they may be related'?"

"You can take that as a *no comment*." Albright said, his jaw thrust toward the TV reporter.

There was a rumble of inaudible conversation coming from the back of the room.

"Ladies and gentlemen," Albright said. "I think this wraps up our session here today."

Schweikert moved quickly to the podium. Albright gave him a look but moved aside. Schweikert said, "We want everyone to rest assured there is no danger to the citizens of our fine county, and we will apprehend the person or persons responsible for these heinous crimes and prosecute them fully."

There were still muffled comments from the rear of the room as if the press conference, or town meeting or whatever it was, had ended too abruptly. But the reporters appeared to have realized they had gotten as much as they were going to get and they began to file out.

Taking advantage of the shuffling of people, I eased toward the rear of the room. I wanted to go to the back of the room and hang around, listen to what was being said there, listen to those undertones, those murmurings. There was something going on with the people there that was not at all friendly to the sheriff and his administration.

Making my way to the back, one hand in my pocket, being casual and speaking to one or two people who were leaving, I glanced over my shoulder at the podium. Schweikert talked to the sheriff and Deputy Wright stood to one side. Linda Shackleford had come forward and apparently thanked the sheriff for the press conference. He gave a tired but friendly smile and shook her hand. Then the sheriff and his group exited the rear door they had entered.

I was now at the back of the room. Five or six people clustered loosely together. The tall man with the narrow face spoke to Patsy. "Your statement came across forcefully, Ms. Davies."

So that was her name. Now I remembered it; she had been quite vocal on a number of issues, mostly those affecting Southern Shores I recalled. The tall man I still didn't recognize. He was dressed casually but didn't look "beachy" to me. Not Outer Banks. His accent, too, was not local—but, heck, more than half the people one met here at the Outer Banks were not local. Ohio, maybe; Pennsylvania? He was apparently, however, a friend or acquaintance of Boyd Bruton, who stood there with me, his middle stuck out comfortably, his small eyes alert and taking everything in.

"Sheriff Albright is a very nice man, a real gentleman," Boyd Bruton said, "but maybe it is just time for a change. More of a take-charge lawman with real experience."

Patsy gave him a quick smile. "You mean like Mr. Ricker, here?"

The tall man acknowledged Patsy's remark with a pleasant nod in her direction.

"We would be well served," Boyd said. "Russ Ricker has had lots of law enforcement experience—and success, I might add—up in the Reading area. And he's been a friend for years."

"Thank you both," Ricker said. He smiled again, but appeared nervous, uncomfortable about something. He shifted his tall frame from one foot to the other.

Okay, Pennsylvania accent. I was right. I stood far enough away from them that they didn't feel I was part of their little group, but I was close enough that I could watch and listen.

Then Ricker said, "But you know I'm not registered here, and there's such a thing as an election, you know." He swallowed and his Adam's apple went up and down.

Patsy gave a short chuckle. "But you're a friend of Boyd's, visiting him, and believe me, he can work things here on the islands."

Boyd started to say something but one of the county commissioners approached him, shook his hand, and said, "You going to be Santa Claus again this year at the parade?"

Boyd bobbed his head and gave out with a "ho, ho, ho." They all laughed. "Then at the Christmas Shop," he added.

When the commissioner went on his way, Boyd said to Patsy, "See, I'm best known as Santa Claus. Not a mover and shaker."

I don't know. I wasn't so sure. There was something going on with the three of them. It was as if they had plans that hadn't quite been verbalized. They had come down from the Southern Shores or Martin's Point at the north end of the Outer Banks, the twenty-five miles down to Manteo for this meeting. It was important to them. It had to be. And I think it was Patsy who served as spokesperson to test the waters about dissatisfaction with Sheriff Albright.

Chapter Thirteen

I had a good excuse now to catch up with Balls, give him a rundown on the press conference as he had requested. It was almost lunchtime and I wanted to speak to Elly before I headed back toward Southern Shores. Not time for lunch, though. Not now.

Hurrying downstairs I stuck my head into Elly's office. And stopped abruptly. There was that damn Gregory Loudermilk leaning one arm casually on the counter while he talked and smiled at Elly. He looked neatly groomed and perfect, naturally. She was behind the counter with one of the large deed books open. She glanced up at me, smiled broadly.

Loudermilk saw Elly's smile and turned to face me. He extended his hand. We shook hands and I said, "Gregory."

He said, "Make it Greg, please, Mr. Weaver."

I nodded. "Greg," I repeated. "And please make it Weav. You can forget the mister bit." I realized I was a bit older than Loudermilk, but I didn't want him emphasizing it. I'm eight years older than Elly. Well, almost nine years older. But most of the time I don't think about that.

He smiled with those perfect teeth like he was proud of them. And he probably was.

Elly spoke up. "Gregory . . . Greg is a history buff also. He wants to start a local history club. For those of us who have an interest in history." She smiled and nodded her agreement.

He said, "I majored in history at William and Mary—before I went to UVA law school. And I know Elly here is a history major also. Seems logical that we start an Outer Banks History Club." He bobbed his head in approval of what he had said.

"My interest is more ancient world history," Elly said, "and Greg's interest is more current—the Lost Colony and all of that—but the idea sounds intriguing."

I saw Elly's coworkers, Becky and Judy, eyeing me seriously. No smiles. Sort of don't-let-him-horn-in looks, if I interpreted their expressions accurately.

"Well, that sounds . . . sounds really good," I managed to say. "It could be fun."

"I don't know if history is ever really what you'd call 'fun,' but it gives one a clearer perspective on what our present condition portends," Loudermilk said. "That's the benefit of history." He blessed me and then Elly with one of his smiles.

Elly said, "Greg wants to take me to lunch to firm up plans for a history club." She gave me a look. "Would you like to join us?"

"I'd love to," I lied, "but I've got to report to Balls . . . SBI Agent Twiddy about the press conference that was just held upstairs." I shifted my weight a bit. "So I've got to run. Just wanted to say hello."

"Call me later," she said. She kept her eyes on me.

I nodded. I also nodded at Loudermilk. "Good luck on the club," I said, and I tried to sound like I meant it.

The wind was cold and I hunched my jacket more tightly across my chest, hands thrust deep in the pockets. I strode fast toward my car, my head down against the wind and feeling a touch of—what was it?—jealousy? Well, I reasoned with myself, certainly no harm in Elly getting more involved in a project like a history club; in fact it'd be good for her, and I know she would enjoy it. Yes, I had to admit it was a good idea—as long as there were a number of other people participating and not just that guy Loudermilk.

As I sat in my car and started the engine, I had to smile at myself, at my reaction to having Mr. Perfect's offer to take Elly to lunch. Yes, I did feel a touch of jealousy. No question about it. I shook my head and eased the car forward. I thought I was through with that sort of thing. Obviously not. I almost chuckled to myself. Well, maybe time to lay more of a firm and binding claim to Elly. Wedding bells? I set my jaw and smiled with determination there in the privacy of my automobile. By golly, she was mine, and I wasn't going to let Mr. Perfect, or anyone else, make any moves.

Driving back across the sound and then up the Bypass, I forced myself to get over the presence of Loudermilk. I was definitely not going to give into unreasoned jealousy. I'm above that, I told myself. Deliberately, I turned my thoughts to the press conference and how little was actually said. The most interesting thing, of course, were the comments from the back from Patsy Davies, and the unmistakable murmurs of discontent with the overall law enforcement, specifically with Sheriff Albright.

And just who was this Russ Rickert? Was he someone Bruton was grooming to make a run for sheriff? Seemed unlikely since Rickert didn't even live here, and with no name recognition at all, he would certainly be a long shot. Whatever his role, he didn't appear all that comfortable with it.

When I arrived at The Marketplace, a tow truck from Seto's Towing Service was lifting the BMW, preparing it to be taken away. The SBI lab van was off to one side. One of the ambulances was still in place, the rear door open and Dr. Willis just emerging. Balls helped him down a step. Officers were removing the yellow tape. Balls spoke to Dr. Willis as I parked nearby and moved quickly toward them. They shook hands and Dr. Willis went to his car. Balls had started to the SBI lab van when I caught up with him.

He stopped, gave me a neutral look.

"Wrapping it up?" I said.

He shrugged and nodded.

"Lab guys make progress?" I indicated the van with a tilt of my head.

"Yeah," he said. "They got the weapons in there, and with computers and stuff they've already run sheets on the two guys. And, yep, just as I thought, they're in the system . . . and have been in it for some time. Hit men, I'm sure of it. From around Philadelphia."

He had removed his heavier winter jacket but still had on his tan sport coat. His shirt was open at the neck. Despite the chilling wind, traces of perspiration dotted his forehead. The sun was trying to break out from the leaden clouds. The forecast called for subsiding winds later today as the low pressure moved farther out to sea. Temperature would rise with a breeze in from the southwest. But now it was still cold.

He gave a wry smile. "Both had handguns with them in the front seat."

"But neither of them had drawn their weapons," I said.

"Nope."

"Obviously they weren't expecting something."

"The one on the passenger side was positioned as if he might have tried to draw. But not enough time."

"Window down. They were greeting someone . . . who turned on them. Suddenly. Without warning."

"That's the way I figure it." He puffed out a sigh. "Press conference? Anything?"

I told him how it went, with emphasis on the group at the back essentially calling for a replacement for Sheriff Albright.

Balls shook his head, whether in disgust or disbelief, I couldn't be sure. He said, "Albright's a good man."

"I know." The wind was already dying down somewhat, or maybe we were just protected by the buildings and trees.

"So what now?" I asked.

He didn't even act like he heard me. Then, "Huh?"

"What now?"

Gazing off into the distance beyond me, he mused, "And just who were these guys expecting? Why would someone do them?" His focus came back to me but I didn't feel like he really saw me. "Had to be someone they trusted. But why do them? Why would the person want to get rid of them? If it was someone they trusted, maybe it was the same guy who hired them. Then get rid of them, but why? They wanted more money?" He shook his head. "Naw, probably not over money. Could be though. But if they wanted more money and were demanding more, would they have been taken so much by surprise? Doubt it." He worked his jaw as if chewing on something more substantial than just thoughts. "Maybe whoever did it didn't want anyone around loose who knew him, knew who he was."

I said, "Getting rid of anyone who could ID him?" I thought about the frustrated efforts to find out the identity of the top man.

"Possible," Balls said. Then he appeared to end his ruminating, as if he wanted to get back to more specifics. He checked his watch. "I wondered why I was hungry," he said.

"Yes, a bit past normal lunchtime."

"Shit, let's get something to eat." He looked around The Marketplace. "Over there?" he suggested, indicating Bonnie's Bagels.

"Sure," I said.

"Let me check with the lab guys. I think they're about ready to head back to Elizabeth City."

When he came back from the SBI lab van, he started to walk the one hundred or so yards to Bonnie's, then said, "Move our cars over closer. I may have to scoot out." He turned to his car, stopped, and over his shoulder said, "Odell Wright or anybody say anything about finding Willie Boy Applewaite?"

"No." I said. "You don't think he had anything to do with . . ." I twisted my head toward the area we were leaving.

"Nope," he said. "Just wondering what's become of him."

At Bonnie's, we took our Cuban sandwiches to one of the tables. Balls had a soda and I had black coffee. He sat facing the front door. Bonnie left the register for a quick visit with us. She stood there shaking her head. "I can't believe what happened out there," she said. "When I came in at five this morning, I saw that car parked there, but I didn't pay any attention to it." She shook her head again and gave a little shiver.

"Bizarre," I agreed. I was just before introducing Balls to her when she had to scurry back to the register.

We ate without talking a minute or so. Then Balls said, "Albright's a good man. Good sheriff. Nobody can blame him. This whole thing is a puzzler." He wiped at his mouth, more or less successfully, with one of the three or four paper napkins he'd pulled from the dispenser on the table. "It'll break though, soon. Too much is happening for it not to." He gave a wry twist to his mouth. "And probably ain't over yet, either." He frowned. "Not finished yet in somebody's mind. I've got a feeling about that." He nodded and took another bite. Half of his sandwich was already gone.

He eyed me from over the top of his soda. "Your theories?"

I picked a tiny piece of the Cuban sandwich that had come loose, lifted the bread and stuck the piece back inside the sandwich. All of this, perhaps, as a way of stalling while I formulated a response. Something I had been thinking about since coming on the scene this morning. "Okay," I said, "like you noted. These two victims didn't expect something. So it had to be someone they knew and were comfortable with. Who could that be? As you said, probably the person who hired them. And why would he do it? It would have to be tying up loose ends. This person—maybe the head guy?—has hired these two. They are the ones who string Tom Applewaite up on the buoy. They are the ones who ambush your CI, poor Leroy. So they are the only ones with direct contact with the top guy. So? The top guy gets rid of them and then there's nothing left to connect him to all this . . . this 'murder and mayhem,' as my editor says."

Balls had finished his sandwich. He looked at the small portion of sandwich I'd left on my plate. I pushed my plate toward him and he plopped the bite into his mouth. Chewing, with his mustache moving up and down, he said, "My theory too, and as good as any. But that still leaves us not knowing who is really behind all of this."

"A local person," I said. I finished my coffee.

Balls nodded, stared off across the parking lot. "Later today I'll get a full report from the lab. There may have been what was left of a partial palm print on the trunk. Everything was wiped down pretty good. Whether it's enough for them to work with, don't know." He straightened up in his chair, flexed his shoulders. "Meantime, I'm heading to Manteo, talk more with Albright and Odell Wright. Fill them in, see what they're thinking."

He stood, glanced down at the table. "You get this?"

"Already paid it," I said.

"Thanks for the lunch." He rose and lumbered away to his Thunderbird.

"Stay in touch," I called.

He didn't turn around but he gave a nod.

I spoke to Bonnie again before I left. After a while I drove south toward my street. I passed Seto's on the way and saw the BMW stowed to one side of their lot. At my house I trudged up the outside stairs and went in the side entrance. Janey chirped a couple of times, cocked her head, watching me. I mumbled something and went to the chair by the phone and sat heavily. I glanced at the answering machine to see whether the message light blinked. No messages. Good. I closed my eyes and leaned back in the chair.

A short time later, Janey gave a weak peep or two. I opened my eyes. "Yes, Janey, life should be more fun than this."

Then I straightened up and said aloud, "Screw this. I'm going to the beach, Janey, pay my respects to the ocean. Get rejuvenated. Want to see how angry the ocean is with this northeast blow."

I drove down to Ocean Bay Boulevard—a rather fancy name for the little street that led from the Bypass two short blocks to the beach access bathhouse and its wooden walkway to the ocean. No other cars were in the parking lot. Not many folks as foolish as I was on a day like today. I walked past the outside showers beyond the bathhouse, which was built to look like the old lifesaving stations. I could hear the ocean, and I paused and actually listened to it. Living here, we get so used to the pulsating surf that we often don't really hear it as something distinct and different. It's best not to get too used to your environment, I figured; I was determined not to become immune to the wonders around us.

I stood at the end of the walkway and surveyed the ocean. It was angry, all right. Frothy-topped waves smashed against the beach and the big waves stretched out several hundred yards. Waves tossed the coarse brown sand on the beach like it was paste being thrown around. No birds were visible. Then I did see two seagulls swooping toward the water. They changed course and flew back to the west, out of my line of vision. The wind flattened my jacket against my chest. I had put my Greek fisherman's cap back on before I got out of my car, and I tugged the bill down to keep it secure. I have tried in the past to identify the different colors the ocean can take on; sometimes, on pretty days, it reflected blue from the sky far out into the distance, and other times it was the dull color of metal. Today it was a mixture of white at the top of the waves, pewter colored at the bottom of the waves, dark green at places, and then brown and white as it broke on the beach. From behind me, the December sun struggled to free itself from clouds that continued to roll in. By tomorrow, I figured this would be over and the sun would win out, the wind would subside, and the temperature would rise. But now I was getting cold. I breathed in deeply, convinced I could actually smell the salt in the air. I realized I smiled. I hunched my shoulders, hands buried deep in the pockets of my jacket, turned and headed back to my car.

This was a good idea. Coming out here to see how angry the ocean was. It was as if it reflected the outrage of humanity.

Chapter Fourteen

I left the ocean and drove back to my house and called Elly at work. I wanted to make plans for tonight—and see how her lunch went with Gregory Loudermilk. I didn't try to ask her about the lunch. I wanted to appear to be above that. We agreed to go out for a quick dinner. I said, "I'd be happy to take your mother and Martin, also."

"Awfully nice of you to offer. But we'll just make it for two."

"Okay, but you know I've got that Julia Child cookbook now, and this week I want to have all three of you over here for one of my gourmet dinners that I'm determined to cook."

A soft chuckle from her.

"Seriously, I can do it. Used to cook quite a bit."

"Oh, I'm sure you're an accomplished chef, Harrison. I can hardly wait. It'll be a wonderful experience." I could sense the smile on her face as she talked. Not making fun, but more like her fondness for me came across the phone line. Then, with her hand covering the mouthpiece, she said something to one of her coworkers. Back to me, she said, "See you about six?"

"Good," I said and we hung up.

Time to call my editor again, fill her in on the latest. Promise her I'd do a full piece on it when the time came. Meanwhile, I know she wanted that update on the Hampton

Roads murders up in the Newport News area of Virginia. Deadline on that was approaching fast. The conversation went well with Rose Mantelli. She was enthusiastic about the possibility of another book on the rash of killings here at the Outer Banks.

That night Elly and I decided on a meal at Darrell's in Manteo. We'd hardly been seated well to the right at a somewhat secluded table than Elly said, "All right, Harrison, tell me all the latest . . . and how you're not involved at all." She gave that little twist of her mouth, head tilted to one side and eyebrow raised. But still there was a soft twinkle in her eyes.

"I will," I said. "But first don't you want to tell me about the Christmas Shop. You know, how it went this first weekend and all of that?" I took a sip of the water that had been brought to the table as we sat down. "Also, I want to know how your lunch went today with Mr. Perf . . . with Gregory Loudermilk."

"That's known as changing the subject, Harrison."

"Yes, that's true. You're absolutely right."

She laughed. "First, the Christmas Shop. It went well. Everyone there is so nice, so friendly, and I love the place. I even made a few sales. Mr. Greene came by and wanted to know how I was doing."

Elly stopped her conversation as we placed our orders with a youngish woman with short blonde hair who knew Elly. The woman wore jeans and a long-sleeve sweatshirt with Darrell's logo on it. They chatted a moment, and Elly asked her about her son, and the woman, introduced to me as Sharon, in turn asked Elly about Martin. Elly ordered sweet tea and I said I would stick with the water. Elly selected broiled shrimp; I opted for a dozen steamed oysters and house salad.

"That going to be enough?" Elly asked when Sharon went to the kitchen with our orders.

"If not, I'll order another dozen," I said. I took another

sip of my water, put the glass down; saw Elly watching me, waiting. "And your lunch?"

"It was pleasant enough. We ate at that Italian place, La Dolce Vita. Very good, but I couldn't eat one of the big entrees, so I settled for a salad and appetizer."

"And Loudermilk?"

"He ate most of his pasta dish. Not sure what it was."

"What about plans for starting a history club? You talk about that?"

She eyed me. Tilted her had ever so slightly. "Yes, of course we did. He said he has at least three other people who are interested—Gary Allen, Monica Stallings, and somebody else I don't know. He wants to start it next month. He suggested having a meeting maybe in one of the coffee houses or some place like that." She put her hand on the glass of sweet tea, appeared to be studying it. She looked back at me. "His interests are more current than mine." She gave a hint of a chuckle. "I prefer talking about the Punic Wars rather than the Lost Colony."

I said, "What's he like? Loudermilk?"

She eyed me again. "Okay. He's okay. Maybe a little, I don't know, prissy or something."

"Married?"

"No. He hasn't been here very long, not that that has anything to do with it. Mentioned his mother again. She lives in northern Virginia. He's a lawyer, as you know. Real estate law, I gather."

I nodded and didn't say anything.

Elly leaned forward, both of her forearms resting lightly on the table. That tilt of her head again. "Harrison, do I detect just a touch of jealousy? Hmm?" She smiled.

"Well, I don't know," I said, and I felt a little foolish and gave an exaggerated shrug.

Elly straightened up and smiled brightly. "Oh, I think that's sweet. You *are* a little jealous." She reached out and touched my left hand. She kept her hand on mine as she said,

"I'm yours, Mr. Crime Writer. You know that."

Without raising my head, I cast my eyes upward, a rather hangdog smile beginning to creep across my face. I was about to say, "And I'm yours," when Sharon bustled up with our food.

Elly's shrimp looked great, and so did my steamed oysters. As she placed the platter with the oysters in front of me, Sharon said, "They're from Crab Slough. Really fresh . . . and certainly local."

The oysters were plump, and yes, in two of the half-shells, were tiny pale crabs nestled next to the host oyster. Crab Slough got its name for a justifiable reason. You ate the miniscule crabs right along with the oyster.

Elly nibbled on one of her shrimp. She inclined her head toward me and said, "And . . . ?"

"And what?"

"You were just about to tell me the latest . . . about what happened up at Southern Shores when you very skillfully changed the subject."

"Okay," I said, and plopped another oyster in the drawn butter, cocktail sauce, and then straight into my mouth. "Well, you heard about the two men who were killed up at The Marketplace, Southern Shores, and I'm sure Mabel gave you a rundown on the so-called press conference . . . so I guess you want to know what Agent Twiddy thinks—it's his investigation—and whether I have any theories of my own—although it's certainly not something I'm really involved in."

"Yeah, right," she said. But there was a trace of a tolerant smile hidden there.

Although I was fully aware that Elly would keep everything I told her in strictest confidence, I still was purposefully vague on some of the theories Balls and I had discussed.

Elly started on another of her shrimp. "I gather that neither you or Agent Twiddy think it's over?"

"Well, the investigation is certainly not over."

She sipped her tea, then said, "That's not what I meant,

and you know it, Harrison."

"Hope the killings are over. But can't be sure, of course."

She stared straight at me. "What about Willie Boy Applewaite? What's happened to him? He can't just . . . just disappear like that."

I nodded in agreement. "Yes, that worries me."

We continued eating in relative silence. Two other couples came in and were given a table but not too close to us. Elly smiled at one of the couples and said she was glad to see them. The woman Elly had spoken to said, "You two going back to Paris again soon?"

Elly smiled. "Love to," she said, "but no plans yet."

The past spring, along with Balls and his wife Lorraine as "chaperones," Elly and I had gone to Paris for nine days. Wonderful time, and we did want to go back.

The two couples began responding to Sharon, who stood at their table with order pad in hand.

To me, Elly said, "I have been thinking about Paris a lot." She gave a short laugh. "In fact the other night I dreamed about Paris."

"What was the dream?" I asked.

She smiled and shook her head. "After listening to my coworker Judy talk endlessly about her dreams, I've sworn I'll never talk to anyone about my own dreams." She leaned forward slightly and confided: "Nothing, absolutely nothing, is more boring than other people's dreams."

I'd never thought about it—until then. "You're right," I said. We both chuckled a bit.

Then, with hardly a pause in between, our gazes locked into each other, and I knew that thoughts of Paris and being together day and night dominated us. I reached over and touched her hand. "Can we drive up to my house and try to pretend we're back in Paris?"

Elly squeezed my hand in return. "We can pretend," she said softly.

We didn't talk much after that, concentrating instead on finishing our meals. Anticipation built in both of us.

Sharon brought the check when I signaled her. "Don't rush off," she said. "How about dessert? Coffee?"

"We're fine," I said. "Just fine. And thanks. It was all good." I nodded as I spoke. Elly had already risen from her seat. We went out together and got in my car. Again, we said very little on the drive across the bridge and heading up the Bypass to my little blue house in Kill Devil Hills. At one point Elly laid her hand lightly on my thigh. I put my hand on top of hers and applied pressure. The tension was there and seemed to be almost palatable between us.

I parked under the carport at my house and we wasted no time in going up the stairs on the side to the kitchen door. I managed to get the door unlocked with a minimum of fumbling. Just inside the door I put my arms around Elly, pulled her to me, and began kissing her. Her lips parted as if she was as hungry as I. We stood there, the kiss growing in intensity.

Janey chirped several times.

We broke the embrace. "Hush Janey," I said.

I took Elly's hand and led her into the bedroom. We clutched each other again, at the same time kicking off our shoes and we parted long enough to begin getting undressed. I almost stumbled getting out of my slacks, and laughed about that. Still smiling, I said, "In the movies they take off their clothes without practically falling over."

"This is more real, though," she said, and she slipped out of her little cotton panties.

Elly stood there, the light from the lamp in the living room casting a glow over her body.

"You're lovely," I whispered. "Beautiful. Delectable."

She came to me and, standing, we pressed against each other. Then we went to the bed. We didn't talk anymore until near the end and I felt Elly tense and she had a very serious expression around her eyes, which were open wide, then closed, and opened again and she lolled her head happily from side to side and said, "Oh, my god . . . oh, my god."

Later, we lay there facing each other, smiles pasted on our faces. She played with the hair on my head and I touched her shoulder. I could tell she was thinking pleasantly about something and getting ready to talk. She propped up on one arm, looked at me, and said, "I know what they talk about when they say something about 'in the heat of passion.' When we were standing there, and you pushed up against me I could feel, really feel, the heat—it was almost hot—the heat in your . . . your . . ."

I gave a bit of laugh. "Don't say 'penis.' I hate that word. It's the wimpiest sounding word in the English language."

She shared the laugh with me. "Okay, Mr. Wordsmith, what word do I use?"

"Oh, anything but penis. Be creative."

She leaned forward and kissed me lightly on the lips. "Some of the slang terms might be better."

"True," I said. Then I propped up on my elbow, looking at her face. "In addition to that being the wimpiest word in the language, practically all of the words for the male genitalia range from being wimpy, to just plain ugly, to sounding like either a joke or a disease." I shook my head in mock disgust. "Terrible names."

She thought about the legitimate terms for the male parts. "I think you're right," she said with a laugh.

I was getting into it. "Now the names for the woman's private parts are, by contrast, pretty and musical sounding. Yes, musical. They sound lovely and have a nice lilt to them."

Her laugh was genuine, and she shook her head in enjoyment. Then she leaned over and peeked at the illuminated bedside clock. "Well, Maestro, I'd better cover my musical body parts with clothing and let you take me home. Do have to work tomorrow."

When we were dressed and went out into the living room, Janey eyed us seriously. She made a soft chirping sound with her throat puffed out, then said quite clearly, "Bitch."

With hands on her hips, Elly gave the parakeet an exaggerated, "Well. Same to you, you smart-aleck."

Janey bobbed her head and said her other word: "Shit."

I took Elly home and stepped inside for a moment. Mrs. Pedersen watched television in the living room with the volume turned low. Several of Martin's coloring books were stacked neatly on the coffee table. He has as many coloring books as Elly does crossword puzzles. She also has a bookcase almost filled with history books dealing with medieval times, her major at Meredith College. I thought about the possibility of a history club, and, yes, it would be nice for her.

I gave her a hug and very discrete peck of a kiss there in the living room and said goodnight to the two of them.

As I opened the front door to leave, Mrs. Pedersen said, "Going to be warm again tomorrow, or at least less cold as this front moves on off." Like everyone at the Outer Banks, weather is much more than just a casual topic of conversation. Keeping an eye on the weather, and being attuned to signs of change, must be an inbred trait of the Outer Bankers.

As I drove away from Elly's, I could feel that the wind had subsided, but it was still there, and my headlights caught leaves scuttling across the road. The question Elly posed at dinner came back to me. She had asked about Willie Boy Applewaite and what has happened to him. Call it a premonition or whatever you'd like, but I had that sinking feeling in the pit of my stomach that brought on a sense of sadness about Willie Boy. I knew something was wrong. There was a reason he hadn't shown up or been found. And it wasn't good.

It wasn't good at all.
I knew that deep down in my soul.

Chapter Fifteen

There was indeed a remnant of December chill in the air when I waked on Tuesday morning. I bumped the heat up a bit. It made the house smell funny for a short period as the system cranked itself on. I uncovered Janey's cage and replenished her seed tray and water. Using the Dust Buster, I sucked up seed hulls that she managed to spread outside of her cage. "How do you do that, Janey?" I said. She enjoyed the noise of the vacuum and the fact that I was speaking to her. She entertained me with her head-bobbing dance, and even did a rather awkward somersault off the inside of her cage. I reached in her cage and picked her up in my hand, cuddling her against my cheek. She likes that, or at least tolerates it. Unlike the male parakeets I've had in the past, she prefers to stay in her cage. She doesn't want to fly around the room and inspect everything like the males did. She's more of a homebody. And very well behaved with the exception of the two words she mimics. I put her back in her cage, and she groomed her feathers, smoothing them down where I had ruffled them holding her.

I stood at the sliding glass doors and looked out at the morning. The sun had broken through clouds that moved ahead of the southwest breeze. Warming up again. As they say here, if you don't like the weather, just wait a few minutes and it'll change. So true.

"Okay, Janey, on this December day I'm going to get back to practicing the bass and finish that article for Rose. How about that?"

She chirped and turned her head from side to side.

"And in addition, I'm not going to be calling Balls to see what's going on. I'm going to stay out of his investigation today, leave him alone."

"Shit," Janey said.

I laughed aloud. "Oh, you don't believe me?"

"Shit," she said again, her head bobbing up and down.

But I stuck to my plan, and after a light breakfast of half a bagel with cream cheese and a microwaved precooked sausage patty, I checked the tuning on my bass and played scales with the bow, slowly and without vibrato. Then, playing pizzicato, I practiced twelve measure blues in several keys. And some jazz riffs. This coming Thursday night I'd be playing with the Jim Watson Jazz Combo at Duck Woods Country Club at a special reception someone was having. I had started playing with Jim's group last year. It was fun, as long as we didn't do it too much. Jim played trumpet, good midrange jazz, and we had an excellent drummer, Bert Campert, and now a new piano player, with whom I'd not played yet but Jim says is excellent. His name is Paul Settlemyer and he recently moved to the Outer Banks. We were lucky to grab hold of him.

When I first started with the group, I had real mixed feelings because I had played with small bands in the Washington area, when my late wife, Keely, sang with many of the groups. I was afraid it would make me sad to be playing again, remembering her and how she sank deeper and deeper into depression, until finally she killed herself. I've had a difficult time coming to grips with that but now, after a little more than three years, I feel that I've moved on. Just the same, when we play some of the tunes that she was so good on, like "Cheek to Cheek," a wave of melancholy will sweep over me right in the middle of the tune. I enjoyed playing with Jim Watson's combo. We only played about once, maybe twice, a month. This was plenty for me. I had no desire to play more regularly in some smoky nightclub until all hours. Been there, done that. Don't want it again. A few short, upscale gigs are fine.

I practiced a good thirty minutes. Laid the bass down, fixed another cup of coffee, and took it outside on the deck. "Still too cold out here for you, Janey," I said. It was in the fifties; it might bump close to sixty by mid-afternoon. The sky had cleared even more, with the southwest wind moving the few, high puffy clouds toward the ocean.

Before I got to work on that article for Rose, I thought about my promise to have Elly, Mrs. Pedersen, and Martin over here for a meal I'd cooked. Friday would be a good time. I couldn't remember whether I had mentioned a specific evening to her. So I went back inside and called the Register of Deeds' office. Becky answered, and I asked if Elly was too busy to come to the phone. In a teasing sing-song voice, Becky said, "She's never too busy to talk to you."

"Thanks," I said, but she had already put the phone down and I heard her say, "Elly, there's someone special on the phone for you."

Elly picked up the receiver. "Hello, someone special."

"Fun time at the Register of Deeds office?"

"Not too busy," Elly said. "Judy was just telling me about her dreams last night."

"Oh, I know that was scintillating."

"Absolutely."

"You know I said I was going to cook dinner for you and your mother and Martin, and I thought this Friday might work for you."

"Oh, that sounds wonderful. I'll check with Mother, of course. But, Harrison, you sure you want to go through this? I know you can cook—at least I assume you can—so you don't have to, you know, prove something to us."

"I want to do it. Got that new cookbook, a few more

pots and pans, and heck, I'm ready to go."

A short laugh from her. "Okay, my Renaissance man, go for it."

"Good. We'll be talking before that . . . and if I'm lucky, I'll see you before then."

"Absolutely," she said again.

I was feeling good and I went to work on finishing that article set in Newport News. It was more or less writing itself because I knew details that I'd worked out in my mind before I sat down to the computer. In such instances, which weren't all that rare, it was almost like transcribing.

Five miles up the road in Southern Shores, a two-year project of dredging the network of manmade canals was underway. There were seven miles of canals in Southern Shores, and by taking the main canal or any of the tributaries, a boater could reach Ginguite Bay, or creek, as many locals called it, and then out into the broad Currituck Sound. The sound stretched north up into Currituck County, past Duck and Corolla. Heading south and east the sound joined the Roanoke Sound and the Greater Albemarle. A boater could keep going south and eventually reach Oregon Inlet, the tricky gateway to the Atlantic underneath Bonner Bridge.

The dredging work had been a long time coming. And it was expensive. It was the first time the canals had been dredged in the more than twenty years since they were first built. The depth of the canals ran about three feet, and depending on the wind-driven tide, that was enough water for most of the boats to navigate. But now they were being scooped out to a depth of five feet. Many of the residents had boats, most in lifts, docked in their backyards adjacent to the canals.

Dredging the canals was an impressive engineering feat. First, a floating barge with a huge mechanical shovel was moved into place. Its powerful diesel engine made a lot of noise coming up the canal and getting to the spot where it had finished the day before. Because of wildlife and consideration of other things that grew in the canals, dredging was only permitted from late fall until around the end of February.

After the barge with its mechanical shovel was in place, there was more noise from the chug-chug-chugging of another barge—an empty one ready to receive the sand and muck from the big shovel. The shovel scooped up the debris from the canal, swung its arm over the waiting barge and dumped it. Usually a crew of two, including the driver, was on the first barge, and two more men on the receiving barge. When the second barge was loaded down with heaps of muck, sand, and dead vegetation, it made its noisy way back down the canal to a spot where waiting dump trucks were loaded with the canal spoils, and they hauled it away up into a location in Currituck County.

And another empty barge made its way back up to the lead barge, ready to receive another load.

Of muck.

Sand.

Rotted vegetation.

And a dead body.

Chapter Sixteen

Because of the way it twisted upon itself, the body did not appear completely intact when the shovel brought it up. Visible was a leg, an arm and the upper torso, bent forward with the head toward the bottom of the shovel. The rest of the body, if it was all there, was covered with muck.

Brian Crowder, the young man operating the shovel, stopped it in midair. Water and debris dripped off the shovel. He stared at the shovel and said, "Oh, shit!"

The other young man on the lead barge, Justin Dayton, rushed around from the rear of the barge, steadying himself with his right hand on the gunwale, his mouth gaped open, eyes wide and locked on the shovel. "Jesus Christ," he said.

Crowder grabbed his cell phone from the control console. He dropped the phone, picked it up quickly and punched in a number. He had to enter the number twice because he hit two numbers at the same time. His voice was high-pitched and frantic. "Boss," he said, "there's a body in the bucket. I scooped up a body in the shovel." He shook his head violently. "No, no," he shouted. "It's a body. No shit, it's a body." Then, still almost shouting, he said, "Yes, sir. Staying right here. You'll get the police. Get somebody here. Quick."

Justin Dayton, with one hand still on the gunwale, suddenly bent over and began to vomit.

Apparently the two crewmen in the receiving barge didn't know immediately why Crowder had stopped the shovel in midair or what was going on with Justin puking. They cast puzzled gazes at each other but then they saw—hanging there in the shovel an arm and a leg. They scampered quickly up to the bow and stood there, mouths open and eyes affixed on the shovel, at the body hanging there. They yelled something at Crowder but he acted like he didn't hear them above the chug-chugging of the idling diesel engines. Actually Crowder heard them asking what in the hell was going on, but he was so frozen in place, his heart still beating so fast in his chest, that he didn't want to respond. He felt that, crap, they could see what was going on. There was a damn dead body in the dredge barge's shovel.

The barges were opposite a vacant house on the west side of the canal, and an empty lot on the other side. The two crewmen on the receiving barge stood around and smoked cigarettes, and except for every now and then tried not to look at the remains of the body suspended high in the air in the shovel. Justin sat on the gunwale of the lead barge, his head bowed low toward his knees, trying not to throw up again. The dripping from the shovel had slowed, but seepage still splashed steadily into the canal. The crewmen kept the barges' diesels idling; they couldn't hear the dripping of the seepage.

The first to arrive on the scene were two uniformed officers from Southern Shores. They had parked a cruiser high in the driveway of the vacant house and scurried to the backyard and stood on the bulkhead of the canal and, with lips clamped tight, gazed up at the shovel and the arm and leg hanging off the lip. From their angle, they could see part of the torso. They couldn't tell whether a head was attached. One of the officers spoke into a handheld radio. Then he signed off and called to Crowder. "You got to stay right there."

Crowder nodded, and flipped a cigarette butt into the

canal. His face was pale and he looked like he might be sick also.

Both of the officers cast their eyes at the shovel and shook their heads. The younger of the officers hurried back to the cruiser and returned with a camera. He began taking pictures from as close as he could get to the edge of the canal.

Two houses up, a man came into his backyard and peered down at the scene. He twisted his head from side to side as if trying to get a better look at what was going on. He walked closer to the edge of his property. His mouth was open and he called something to the officers or to Crowder, but the sound of his voice was muffled by the idling diesels. One of the officers shrugged and held a hand up to his ear indicating he couldn't hear—or didn't want to.

In just a few minutes, three other uniformed Southern Shores police arrived. They had pulled a cruiser into the backyard of the vacant house, slightly ahead of the first vehicle. One of the uniforms was the Southern Shores chief, Curtis Durwood.

The four officers gathered close to Chief Durwood, while he studied the shovel's contents, a deep frown on his face.

Durwood's voice was a little unsteady as he said, "We can't leave it—or him—hanging up there in the shovel. They're going to have to load it into the barge. Jeeze, and see whether there's anything else down there." He shook his head. "Oh, my God. Never seen anything like this." He acted like he tried to spit. "Jeeze, and this on top of those two slain in The Market Place. What the hell's happening here in Southern Shores?" He had been police chief in Southern Shores less than two years. In that time, there had only been a few incidents of vandalism, two thefts of phones or audio equipment stolen out of unlocked vehicles, and other minor infractions. Nothing like this.

The chief called to the crewman of the lead barge. "We're getting someone else here and we'll have to get a police boat or Coast Guard Auxiliary boat up here and you're going to have to put it, you know, in the other barge."

Crowder either didn't hear everything the chief said, or he didn't want to believe it.

"Stay? Like we are?"

"Yes, son. We'll tell you what to do next. We got to have some help first." The chief studied the situation. He chewed on his lower lip. Then he called to Crowder again. "Dump the contents in the barge, and then the barge driver can bring it over to the bulkhead so we can board."

The older of the uniformed officers stood close to the chief and said, "Sir, had maybe we better get more pictures of the body and all before they dump it on the other barge?"

The chief mulled that over and then nodded his head. He called to Crowder: "Don't dump the body yet. Swing the shovel as close this way as you can so we can get more pictures."

The officer with the camera stood at the ready, his feet slightly apart as if bracing himself, as the shovel moved steadily toward the bulkhead. Crowder stopped the shovel's forward movement, and he lowered it a few feet.

"That's close enough," the chief yelled.

The officer with the camera compressed his lips and began taking pictures. He looked back at the chief and said, "I think I've got enough." Distress was etched on the young officer's face.

The chief nodded.

A woman and another man had come out into the backyard of the house where the first man had stood. The woman put her hand over her mouth and turned away. Two dogs were with them and both dogs began barking.

Crowder shook his head, more in disbelief than a signal he wasn't going to comply. "Okay," he said.

The chief yelled back at him. "But keep your barge in

place. You may have to dig down some more, see if there's anything else down there." Chief Durwood continued to chew his lower lip. As if talking as much to himself, he said, "We'll maybe get a diver to search the bottom . . . or maybe the Coast Guard."

Crowder's body language acknowledged he understood; he took a deep breath, and moved slowly into the pilothouse. Crowder put his hands on the control levels. The shovel arm swung up and then around and halted close to the bow of the waiting barge. The two crewmen on the waiting barge moved all the way to the stern, getting as far as they could away from the shovel. They kept their gaze locked on the shovel and its contents.

Crowder positioned the shovel low over the bow of the barge, and released its maw. The muck and the body tumbled onto the barge. The barge crewmen stayed in the stern, but their eyes were trained steadily on the deposit.

The chief watched the operation, standing with his fists clenched by his side. After the shovel emptied, the chief yelled to the driver of the receiving barge, "Now see if you can maneuver over here to the bulkhead so we can board."

"Yes, sir," the driver said and he stepped behind the controls of the barge. The engine became loud. He bumped the barge into reverse and then inched it slowly forward and to the west and got it along side the bulkhead. The other crewman on the receiving barge threw a line to one of the officers who secured it to a piling.

An officer stood beside Chief Durwood as he prepared to take a long stride from the bulkhead onto the gunwale of the barge. The officer held one of the chief's arms as he got aboard. Then the chief turned and helped the officer join him.

From what Durwood could see as they approached the muck-covered body was that it was mostly intact. But one arm did appear to be missing. Maybe it was just covered and twisted around. They didn't move anything. The head of the body was still attached but covered with sand and rotted vegetation.

"Oh, Lord," the chief said, his voice low and not very even. "We got to get some people here," he said. The officer with him nodded and swallowed as if bile had risen into his throat. The chief continued: "Get the county involved, the coroner, and the SBI, maybe the Coast Guard . . . some more help."

Durwood pulled a handkerchief from his pocket and covered his nose. He bent forward to get a closer look at the body. He pointed to a cinder block that was tied snug to the body's upper thigh. The chief straightened his stance, shook his head and turned his back to the body. He removed a cell phone from his belt, and began one of several quick conversations. He replaced his cell phone.

Crowder, the crewman on the barge with the shovel, called, "You still want me to stay right here?"

"Yes," the chief yelled. "Be prepared to dig some more when I tell you."

The crewman nodded, but didn't appear pleased with the order.

Within several minutes, more officers arrived, plus an emergency vehicle; neighbors from nearby houses had come into their backyards to gawk at the activity and talk among themselves.

Alerted by the phone call from the Southern Shores chief, Dare County Sheriff Albright sped northward on the Bypass toward the scene in a cruiser driven by Deputy Odell Wright. Dr. Willis, the coroner, sat scrunched down in the backseat, appearing not at all comfortable with how fast they drove, lights flashing, siren screaming. Trailing them, SBI Agent Ballsford Twiddy's classic Thunderbird, a blue light flashing from its grille and from a light affixed on the roof, kept within a few yards of the cruiser.

Chapter Seventeen

Although the wind was down, it was cold standing around at the canal. The crewmen and the officers stood with shoulders hunched up toward their necks, windbreakers and jackets drawn up tight. Shadows lengthened as the afternoon sun touched the tops of tall pines in Southern Shores.

About two hours of daylight remained when Sheriff Albright, Deputy Wright, Dr. Willis, and Agent Twiddy arrived. The driveway of the vacant house was full so they pulled their vehicles up on the lawn, as close into the backyard as they could get without driving over shrubbery.

Balls and the sheriff strode quickly toward the bulkhead. Deputy Wright walked more slowly, favoring Dr. Willis.

Southern Shores Chief Durwood and the other officer had gotten off of the barge and stood near the water's edge. They turned as Balls and Albright approached.

"Glad you're here, Sheriff," the chief said. He nodded toward Balls, extended his hand, "You too Agent Twiddy. Glad to have the SBI assistance on this investigation. Happy to turn the whole damn thing over to you." Then he pursed his lips, frowned and cocked his head to one side, and added, "As much as I can since it's in my backyard, so to speak."

Balls kept his gaze on the barge.

"We've been aboard," the chief said. "But we didn't try to move anything. Wanted to wait until . . ." He inclined his head toward the approaching Dr. Willis, ". . . until everyone was here. Get it documented, so to speak."

Balls said, "I thought the body was in the . . ." He nodded toward the shovel. ". . . in the shovel."

"It was," Durwood said, "when it was dug up. But we thought we'd better get a look at it, so I had them dump it right there."

Balls glared at Chief Durwood, his jaw clamped tight, but didn't say anything.

"We didn't disturb anything," Durwood said, shifting his eyes to Sheriff Albright and back briefly to Balls.

Balls stood there a moment or two, surveying the scene. He took in the neighbors standing at the edge of their property conferring with one another. Now there were three dogs with them, barking at the activity. Irritably, Balls muttered, "Wish they could shut those dogs up." He took a couple of steps to the bulkhead. "Between those diesels and those dogs, ain't exactly a peaceful scene is it?" Deputy Wright, who had come up beside Balls, nodded his head in agreement.

"Nope," Balls said, "not peaceful at all." He gave a mirthless short chuckle. "Murder scene's not the most peaceful place anyway, don't suppose." He turned to Wright. "Let's take a look." Balls stretched a leg up on the gunwale and accepted the helping hand of one of the crewmen.

Albright came next. The sheriff turned back to Deputy Wright. "You can stay there for right now," he said. "Help Dr. Willis aboard when it's necessary."

"Yes, sir," Wright said.

Dr. Willis clasped the fastenings on his jacket, turned the collar up and rested by leaning against one of the pilings. "Still cold out here," he muttered to no one in particular.

Balls and the sheriff took their time approaching the bow of the barge. Balls' gaze took in everything around them. They stepped carefully along the edge of the barge, getting close to the bow. Balls was in the lead, and he continued a few steps beyond Albright so that he was actually on the very front end of the barge, looking back at the body. From where he stood, he could see more of the torso, the head, and the muck-stained face.

He shook his head sadly. To Albright he said, "Well, one of the mysteries has been solved. We know where Willie Boy Applewaite is." His voice was tight, controlled, and just loud enough to be heard above the idling diesels. "He's right here. What's left of him." The wind from the southwest carried the odor away from Balls, but the smell reached Albright and he covered his nose with a large handkerchief.

Albright kept the handkerchief up to his face. Balls watched him. Albright wouldn't turn back to Willie Boy's body, and Balls was quiet. His head down, Albright said, "I loved those boys. I wanted to keep them out of trouble, for their daddy's sake if nothing else. They were not bad boys. Just . . . just, I don't know." He turned and looked toward Balls. Albright's eyes were moist and there was also a growing anger in his countenance. "We've got to wrap this investigation up, Agent Twiddy. We've just got to."

Balls nodded but didn't say anything.

Balls held one hand out toward the shore. "Camera," he said. The officer with the camera started to come aboard. Instead, he passed the camera to the outstretched hand of the crewman, who passed it to Albright. Balls stared at the body until Albright inched forward and put the camera in Balls' hand. Balls glanced at the camera and saw how to operate it. He took several pictures from slightly different angles, moving to the right and left, but remaining on the end of the bow. He secured the camera strap around his neck. He turned toward Dr. Willis, who continued to lean against the piling, head tilted down toward his feet.

To Albright, Balls said, "Sheriff, please see if any of your men or these other officers have some, you know, boots or something that Dr. Willis can put on. Lot of crap up here. And he's gonna have to take a look."

Sheriff Albright called to Deputy Wright and made the request. There was some conversation among the officers and then one of the EMTs from the emergency vehicle hurried away and came back with high boots and an orange rubberized suit to wear around hazardous material. Dr. Willis looked in astonishment at the garb as they approached him with it. But he complied and the officers and the EMT began helping him suit up. It was all too big for him, and except for the gruesome nature of what he was preparing to do, it would have been comical. He waddled toward the barge and Deputy Wright and another officer helped him get aboard the barge. Sheriff Albright and the barge crewman helped from the gunwale.

Dr. Willis had also donned latex gloves and he tucked the wrist openings over the tops of the long orange sleeves of his rubberized suit. Balls steadied the doctor as he stepped over the lip of the barge and prepared to squat next to the body. He gingerly pushed aside some of the muck. Willie Boy's left arm was missing from above the elbow. Dr. Willis studied the stump of arm, then glanced at the teeth on the barge's shovel. The shovel was suspended a few yards above them and back toward the lead barge.

In addition to the one cinderblock that was secured to the upper thigh, another cord was around his torso but there was not a cinderblock attached. Dr. Willis made no comments but his grim countenance said it all as he went about his gruesome task of examining the body as much as he could. Balls leaned forward, his hands resting on the lip of the barge's receiving area. He had picked a spot that was relatively clean, but before he put his hands down he brushed at the lip and then wiped his palms on his slacks.

Balls watched Dr. Willis, straining to hear anything he might say. "Been dead about three days, maybe four," Dr. Willis mumbled, "best I can tell." He studied Willie Boy's upper chest. "Two gunshot wounds here," he said.

"The arm?" Balls asked. "Shovel do that?"

Dr. Willis said, "I expect it's still down there," he nodded to the canal. "Looks like maybe that shovel cut it off
bringing him up."

Balls turned toward the shoreline. "Chief, see if the
shovel operator can bring up something else. We're missing
part of an arm." He shook his head. "Who knows what else."

The chief called to the shovel operator, but he had already heard and had moved into the pilothouse. The engine
revved and the shovel swung over the canal in front of the
barge. The operator lowered it, dug into the bottom of the
canal, and came up with only muck. He maneuvered the
shovel to the far side of the barge, away from Balls and the
others. He dumped the muck onto the back section of the
barge. He did it again. Nothing but muck. The third time,
though, he brought up the arm and another cinder block, a
short piece of cord tied to the block. Balls and Dr. Willis
watched as the maw of the shovel made its deposit toward
the rear of the barge. The arm was near the top, poking upward out of the muck, the hand aimed at the sky, the fingers
extended as if reaching in supplication.

Dr. Willis shook his head. Some of the officers stared
and then looked away. Two residents of the area had entered
the backyard of the vacant house, but one of the uniformed
officers kept them back, talking quietly to them.

To Albright, Balls said, "We may get a diver to search
around down there. See if they come up with anything else."
Balls straightened, took a deep breath. He rubbed his chin
against a hunched shoulder, as if he tried to wipe it all away.
With a steady gaze, he slowly turned his head, taking in the
areas on both sides of the canal, and the canal itself, which
was a good ten yards wide at that spot. More to himself, he
mused, "How'd they get him here in the canal? Couldn't toss
him in from the side and not enough current to move the
body out in the middle. Have to be a boat. Anyone missing a
boat?"

Balls sighed heavily, and looked down at Willie Boy

Applewaite, a mixture of anger and frustration etching deep lines in his face. "We've got a lot of work to do," he said quietly. Even Dr. Willis couldn't hear him. Didn't need to.

I didn't learn anything about the discovery of Willie Boy until Elly called early that evening. She tried to control her voice but I could hear the quaver in her tone. "They've found Willie Boy Applewaite." A pause. She spoke softly I knew so Martin couldn't hear her. Her words caught as she tried to go on. "Bottom of the canal in Southern Shores." Then there was a soft sob. "They dug him up from the bottom when they were dredging." I heard her breathe. "It's just horrible."

"Oh, Christ," I said.

Her voice was a bit more even, as if by force of will. "Mabel called me." She continued and told me what details she knew, which were sketchy. She did know that he had been shot, and had probably been killed Friday night, maybe Saturday.

I did a quick mental timeline. That would be before the two hit men were killed, which occurred Sunday night or in the wee hours of Monday.

Elly's voice still trembled. "Harrison, what in the world is happening? What's going on? Has the world, the Outer Banks, become a place of horror? I feel like we're in some scary movie and I keep wanting to shut my eyes and not see anymore of it." She was on the verge of crying.

What the hell could I say that didn't sound like a platitude, a meaningless bit of pap? Okay, Harrison, say something to her, I told myself. "It's a war that certain elements are having, Elly. We're just seeing it from the outside, like onlookers watching the battle raging." I don't know where I came up with that crap. But I realized it was the truth. This *was* a war. Not one we were embroiled in, but we were witnesses to it. Maybe Balls and the sheriff and other lawmen were involved, but they were the ones trying to find out who the participants were and stop them.

Then suddenly, while I was verbalizing these things to Elly, it occurred to me that maybe, just maybe, the field was being narrowed, and leading back to the one person responsible. Maybe, just maybe, the killings were over, and now the job focused on one thing: finding the person behind the curtain. The one pulling all of this off.

It was obvious that the citizens on the Outer Banks, and the vacationers who considered it their second home, reeled in shock with what had happened here in less than a week. The deaths—and not just deaths—but the slaughtering, bizarre gangland stuff that as Elly said would only be seen in a graphic movie, not in real life. But this was real life and it had happened here.

Elly held the phone away from her lips but I could hear her clearly: "No, no, Martin. Mama's just fine. I was just . . . a little upset but Mama's fine." I heard a kissing sound. "I'll be in there with you in just a minute. Go back in there with Nana." Then to me, she said, "Please, please, Harrison. Stay out of this . . . if you can. There's something evil out there. I worry. You know I do."

"I know there's evil, Elly." With absolutely as much assurance as I could muster, I said, "But I really believe it will be taken care of, solved. Agent Twiddy and the others won't rest until this is ended."

We said goodnight, uttered terms of love and endearment, and hung up.

I sat by the phone staring across the room. What a hell of few days it had been. I couldn't help but think about my early premonition that the Applewaite brothers were marked for death. Now both of them were gone. Janey chirped once or twice but I ignored her. Had I eaten? No, and I wasn't at all hungry but knew I needed to eat. The easiest thing was cereal. Moving like I was in a trance, I went into the kitchen and fixed a bowl of cereal, poured in milk and loaded the cereal with sugar. I stirred it and ate absently, leaning on the kitchen counter.

I wouldn't bother Balls, not tonight. Maybe in the morning, tomorrow. It'd be Wednesday. The day before the Jim Watson Combo played at Duck Woods, a short distance from where they'd scooped up Willie Boy's body today. I wondered how festive the reception would be. Life goes on, and while I'm sure it would be a topic of conversation, it wouldn't dominate. It was something that happened but didn't concern them that much. There would be laughter and we would play lively tunes and the music would flow.

I watched Janey cocking her head toward me. "Life's a bitch, Janey," I said.

She bobbed her head, glad I was talking to her, and said, "Bitch."

"Yes," I said. "And time for bed. Call it a day."

Chapter Eighteen

Clouds had completely moved out overnight and when I got up Wednesday morning it appeared that NOAA's forecast was correct and that the temperature might get up to sixty degrees. Not as warm as the end of last week, but pretty darn good for December. I uncovered Janey's cage and started coffee and stood at the sink staring out the kitchen window. I could smell the coffee and that helped. Checked the time. Not quite seven-thirty. After the first sip of coffee, I went to the phone and dialed Balls' cell number.

When he barked a "Yeah?" I said, "Well, you've got to eat."

"Huh?"

"Breakfast. It's the most important meal of the day."

"Screw you."

"You been up all night?"

"Just about."

"You sound like it."

"Breakfast? I guess I ought to."

"Where are you?"

"Going over notes. Trying to put things together."

"No, I said where are you?"

"Huh? Oh, still here at the sheriff's office. I think I've been here most of the night."

"How about twenty minutes from now, breakfast some

place? Not the Dunes." I alluded not to the food but to the tragedy that had occurred the other morning when we had dined there and been joined by Leroy, just before he was gunned down.

"They probably got something across the street. Meet you there? You're buying."

"My editor is."

"Everything'll be off the record. Even my hello."

"See you then . . . and there."

There were several parking places right near the courthouse. When I pulled up it was close to eight o'clock. Balls stood outside the courthouse on the sidewalk, peering left and right. Most of the businesses were closed.

"Maybe the Dunes ain't such a bad idea," he said.

"We'll eat here," I said. We went across the street.

After we were seated, and as secluded as we could get, I looked at him and shook my head. "You look like crap," I said. He wore a wind resistant jacket, collar turned up. Smudges of dirt stained the elbows, and there was some of the same soiling on the thighs of his slacks, as if he'd tried to rub dirt from his hands. Overnight stubble was on his cheeks, neck and chin.

"Yeah, thanks." He gave one of his short, mirthless chuckles. "Actually probably look better than I feel." With his thumb and index finger he smoothed out his mustache. It was the best groomed thing about him that morning.

"Any progress?"

Balls shook his head just as the server, a young man who didn't look like he'd had enough sleep either, came to take our orders. I got a couple of eggs over light, ham, toast and coffee. Balls told the young man he wanted a big glass of tomato juice with ice in it, the three-egg cheese and ham omelet, hash browns on the side, an extra order of toast, and plenty of coffee, and to keep the coffee coming. On a much smaller scale, his order was almost identical to my order at Henry's the other morning.

Balls grinned at me. "Remember you're paying." Then his face went serious and weary again, just that quickly.

"The thing with Willie Boy . . ." I said and let the sentence hang there like a question.

He made a face, shook his big head again. "Willie Boy Applewaite was probably the last job those two hit guys pulled before they got theirs as well—and got done in not far from where they'd killed Willie Boy." The server brought two mugs of coffee. Balls began loading his with sugar. "At least I hope it was the last job they pulled." He stirred his coffee. "And I think it was." He took a loud slurp of his coffee, and squinted his eyes as if he stared at a thought in the far distance: "I believe whoever is behind this thinks now he's tied up all the loose ends." Then he got a half-crooked smirk around his mouth. "But that's where he's probably making his mistake. All the loose ends are never tied up. It's like trying to keep frogs in a bucket. Some gonna jump out."

Our food arrived, along with a tall glass of tomato juice with crushed ice and a plate piled high with buttered toast. The server returned in a few seconds with a container of packets of jelly. "Good," Balls said. He dived in. I wasn't far behind.

After a moment or two of eating, I said, "Those two guys from Philadelphia or Reading or wherever they were from, they had to be staying somewhere around here, and I wonder if . . ."

Balls had a mouthful of food but he interjected. "You're behind the curve, Weav. Already checked that out some time—what days, hours, whatever—ago. Deputies took their mug shots around to motels up and down, mostly Kitty Hawk and Kill Devil Hills. Found out in short order where they were staying." He swallowed his mouthful of food and finished washing it down with iced tomato juice. "I interviewed the desk clerk who checked them in, and checked them out." He couldn't help but treat himself to an indulgent half-grin as he thought about the words. ". . . and before they got themselves checked out."

I said, "I'm sure their room or rooms were gone over. Anything?"

"Naw, but here's what's interesting." He thought a moment before he continued, deciding what to tell me, I'm sure. Picking up a half a slice of one of the pieces of toast, he slathered it with grape jelly, folded it into a triangle, and pushed it into his mouth. "The clerk, sort of a nerdy type, said he noticed when he checked them in that they each had one small overnight bag, but when they checked out they had a third bag, and they seemed to debate as to which one of them was to carry it." He cut once more into his omelet, which oozed whey from the cheese, giving an orange tint to his plate. "I asked him how come he could be certain on the number of bags they carried. He said it was sort of a hang up of his. He counted things. Then he said to me, 'Like your jacket has two buttons in the front. Most of the jackets like that I see nowadays have three buttons.' I told him it was an old, old jacket, and that I liked the two buttons."

"I don't see how the number of bags . . ."

Again he continued as I let my statement drift off. "Tell you why I think it's interesting. And this nerdy guy was absolutely sure it was two bags going in and three bags coming out a day or two later." He leaned forward and grinned at me. He loved this sort of thing.

"Yes?" I said.

"When we popped the trunk of that BMW, there were those weapons in there, and that's what most of us were concerned with, but there was something else—only two overnight bags. Not three."

"You think what? Their payoff? Money in the third bag."

He smiled and nodded his head. "The key fob that popped the trunk was lying in the dead driver's lap. Wasn't in the ignition. It was like someone had taken it out, opened the trunk, tossed the key back in the window."

I leaned back, taking this in.

"One other thing. The lid on the trunk had been wiped like someone trying to make sure no prints were there." He permitted himself a bit of a chuckle. "But there was one smudged partial still there. Best our lab guys could do when they went over that car was to declare it was something of a partial, but not enough to do much with . . . and that they couldn't find anything in the system that matched. Best they could do."

"So," I said, "whoever shot them took the money. That what you're saying?"

"Or maybe took *back* the money," he said with a smile. "Once again, tying up loose ends."

I thought about it a moment, stirring the eggs around with my fork. I looked at Balls. He continued eating. I said, "Not too much of a stretch to figure they were waiting there for the big guy, waiting for their final payoff, when—bang, bang—instead of money."

He finished his tall glass of tomato juice and crunched loudly on pieces of ice. "No stretch," he said. "Whatever they were waiting for, they thought it was a friendly visit. Window down, guns not drawn." Balls searched his plate for another scrap of omelet. With a half a piece of toast, he sopped at drippings. "Another thing, about that car."

"The BMW?"

"Yeah. Our guys thought at first that it was a rental from the Norfolk airport. I knew right off that had to be wrong, once I saw all that armament in the trunk. They weren't getting through any airport with all that firepower. No, the BMW was rented from an agency in Philadelphia. They drove down."

The young man brought Balls more coffee. I indicated I was fine.

Balls shifted in his seat and flexed his shoulders. He sighed. Weary. "This gotta break soon. Just has to."

I signaled for the check. "Going back to that clerk at the

motel. Can't help but wonder why he paid so much attention to those two guys."

Balls grinned at me. "You're coming along, Weav. I wondered the same thing, and asked him why. He said because they didn't look or dress like any of the other vacationers he checked in. Dark clothing, somewhat spiffy looking. That's the word he used: 'Spiffy.' Dress shoes that had long pointed toes like French shoes."

I shook my head. "Either that motel clerk is about the most observant character around, or he's got a hell of an imagination."

Balls chuckled. "You'd have to meet the guy. You'd believe him." He stood, and I picked up the check, glanced at it and peeled off a tip for our young server. The server thanked us on our way out, trying his best at the same time to stifle a yawn. He needed to get more sleep.

Outside, Balls cast his eyes skyward at the few puffy clouds that moved from the southwest. "Better," he said, referring I assumed to the weather. His jacket was unzipped. "Thanks for the breakfast," he said.

"Willie Boy?" I said. "Results? Autopsy and stuff."

"Probably killed Saturday night. Two shots up close, in the chest. One went through him. One was lodged in the spine. Slug was pretty well mutilated. Can't tell all that much about it . . . sort of. The other one, hell no way of ever finding it. We don't know where he was actually killed. There at the canal? Wouldn't someone have heard the shots? Unless the killers used a suppressor. Had to be tied up, too. Weighted down. Could have been done at the canal, near that vacant lot? Had to have a boat, I thought at first. So he could be dumped in the canal. But the dredge operator said he couldn't remember whether he dug him up along the side of the canal or in the middle. If the other bullet went in the canal . . . with all that crap in the canal . . ." He turned as if he wanted to get away from me.

I put out a hand and touched his arm. "What do you

mean 'sort of.' And not a small caliber in the back of the
head?"

He got one of those half-grins. "Nope." He hesitated. I
could tell he once again debated with himself as to how
much to say to me, but I knew, too, that he wanted to spring
the information on me, something he enjoyed, like letting the
other shoe drop. "The lab guys haven't finished yet, but preliminary is that the slug in Willie Boy was probably fired
from the same weapon that killed the two guys in the
BMW."

I arched my eyebrows. "Wow," I said. "Mr. Big Guy
gets his hands dirty?" I thought more about it. "But Willie
Boy had those cinderblocks tied to him, and moving him to
the canal, dumping him in. Seems like it would take more
than one guy."

Balls gave a short shrug. "Maybe." He smoothed his
mustache. "Who knows? Maybe someone else is helping
him." He stood there a moment longer, pulled a toothpick
from his jacket pocket and began poking viciously at his
teeth. "Okay," he said, "let's suppose that Willie Boy did
find out who the big guy is, went to him, confronted him,
Mr. Big shoots him, and then gets his two goons to get rid of
the body. Their last assignment for him. They want more
money, and he promises to get it for them. Does them in
instead." He cocked his head to one side, a trace of a smile
beginning, and raised an eyebrow. "Just a theory," he said.

"May be just a theory," I said, "but it makes as much
sense as some of the other stuff."

He shrugged again. "Gotta go," he said. "Remember
everything's off the record. Even 'hello.'"

"You never said hello."

He grinned and was gone.

Chapter Nineteen

Before leaving Manteo, I stuck my head into the Register of Deeds office briefly to speak to Elly. I got there just as she hung up her hip-length navy blue coat. It was the heaviest coat she generally wore during the winter, a wardrobe's concession to more of the past couple of days than today.

"Well, good morning to you, Harrison," she said. "This is a nice morning greeting."

Her coworkers Judy and Becky grinned at the two of us, expectant expressions in their eyes as if they thought they were about to see a passionate embrace. I spoke to them, and they came closer.

"I just had breakfast with Agent Twiddy," I said.

Elly nodded, and eyed me, waiting for me to say something else.

"Just checking with him," I said. "Sort of making sure he takes nourishment."

"Uh-huh," she said and arranged items on her desk, but still eyeing me. Then, more seriously, she asked, "Anything?"

I shook my head. "Nothing."

One of the real estate attorneys came into the office. Elly smiled and came forward to help him. At least it wasn't Gregory Loudermilk.

I nodded a goodbye and gave a quick wave also to Judy

and Becky, and drove back to Kill Devil Hills and my little house. Needed to finish that Newport News article and send it electronically to Rose. By three o'clock I had wrapped it up, saved it in a file, and attached it to an email that I sent. Rose shot a brief note back that it had been received.

I didn't hear anything further that day from Balls, and didn't really expect to. I vowed to leave him alone for a day or two, maybe. No guarantee.

Later in the afternoon I played the bass a few minutes and tried not to think of different theories about the murders. To help accomplish that, I channeled my concentration to what I would cook for Elly, her mother, and Martin on Friday. A trip to Fresh Foods or Harris Teeter would be necessary, but not this evening. I'd wait until Thursday midmorning.

Darkness was coming on but I stepped out on the deck to watch the last of the day. It was quiet back here in my cul-de-sac. High tide was at its peak and I listened intently for the surf a quarter of a mile away. I thought I could hear it, but I wasn't sure. The wind was mild but still moved the branches of the live oak and the scrawny needles of my pine tree. I liked smelling the night's onset, the close of the day.

Thursday morning when I got up and stirred around I knew I needed to get serious about what I would be cooking the next evening. I had perused several recipes in the Julia Child book and, while they sounded delicious, they were also rather complicated for me; I needed more practice, a more extended learning curve. Tomorrow night wasn't enough time. Okay, so I would do something I knew how to do. And off to Fresh Foods I went.

After coming back from the grocery store and putting away the provisions—and a lot of them, and things I would not normally buy—I thought about calling Balls. Heck, it had been more than twenty-four hours since I had last bugged him. Maybe time to do it again. Didn't care whether he barked at me or not.

When he answered, he didn't exactly bark. But he sounded angry, and not directed toward me. "World's filled with people don't have enough to do," he said.

"Well, you know, Balls, they say it takes all kinds."

"No," he said, "it doesn't *take* all kinds, there just *are* all kinds."

"You're right," I said with the hint of a chuckle. "Okay, what's up?"

"A petition," he said. "A petition is being circulated saying Sheriff Albright needs to be replaced and more professionals brought in to curb all the violence in Dare County." He made a dismissive sound, an unintelligible grunt. But his disgust came across clearly.

"Who started that?" I had an idea it might be Patty Davies who was at the press conference.

"Up in Southern Shores," he said.

"Uh-huh. Patty Davies?"

"She's one of them. Also Boyd Bruton, our Santa Claus, and maybe his friend you told me about. Ricker or something. But lots of others have signed on, too, apparently. They took it to the newspaper, and your friend Linda called the sheriff about it. Wanted a comment."

"Linda Shackleford," I said. "But what do they expect? Sheriff's an elected official . . . and a popular one."

"I don't know," he said, the anger still there, but a weariness overriding it. "Probably want to install their own man or woman or something. Not going to get anywhere, but just another distraction for the sheriff and his staff while we're up to our asses investigating."

I almost hesitated to say it, and wish I hadn't, but I said, "No real progress, huh?"

"Whadda you think?" he said.

"Sorry."

"Yeah, me too."

Later that afternoon I showered and got dressed in black slacks, black pullover shirt. This was our uniform, so to speak, for the Jim Watson Combo. I had put my bass in its canvas cover and it lay on the living room floor, looking like a shroud. We were to start playing at seven at Duck Woods Country Club, and I would need to be there shortly after six-thirty. Figured I'd better eat a little something first. Had grapes and other fruit I'd bought at Fresh Foods, so I dived into some of that. Also replenished Janey's seeds and water. Gave her a sprig of millet as a treat.

At close to six, I called Elly at home. "Hope I'm not interrupting anything."

"Oh, no," she said. "I've been home for—I don't know —half an hour or so. I was going to get here in time to help Mother cook supper, but she's already started and shooed me out of the kitchen." I heard Martin in the background saying something. Elly said, "Excuse me . . ." and she spoke to Martin with her hand over the mouthpiece of the phone, but her words were still clear: "I'll be back there in a minute, Martin. Keep coloring." She laughed softly as she came back to me and said, "I'm getting really good at coloring, staying in the lines."

I said, "I wish you were going to be a groupie tonight when we play."

"Me, too," she said. "I like being a groupie, but there at Duck Woods I don't believe I can just breeze into that reception saying, 'I'm with the band.'"

"No, probably not . . . but next time. We've got a gig a few days before Christmas that should work fine for my favorite groupie."

"I better be your *only* groupie."

"You are, you are," I said. We both laughed and I told her I was looking forward to having them over for dinner tomorrow night.

"Now don't try to overdo it, Harrison," she said.

"Well, I want to make it fancy. So I'll probably cut the crust off the bread on the bologna sandwiches."

"Sounds wonderful," she said and we said goodnight.

Before we hung up she said, "Play pretty."

I parked temporarily close to the side door in the upper parking lot of Duck Woods Country Club and slid my bass from the rear of the Outback. I laid the bass on the little porch and then parked my car off to the side. Came back and maneuvered in with my bass, its neck resting on my right shoulder and one arm gripping the shoulder of the instrument. I swear the bass gets heavier each year.

Bert Campert, the drummer, was already inside setting up his drum set. Bert is a big guy, a little heavy, with curly hair that looks like it never needs combing. Jim Watson arranged the music fronts. There were only two of the fronts, one for him and one for me. Bert had a playbook on a stand near his high-hat cymbal. Another playbook would be on the piano. I still called it a piano, although technically it was an electronic keyboard that sounded like a piano. Our relatively new piano player, Paul Settlemyer, had apparently come in just ahead of me. He stood to one side, a rather dreamy expression graced his face. He smiled at me and nodded his head. We stowed cases into a room off to the side that lead back to the kitchen. Our "bandstand" area was free of clutter and looked good. Jim stepped back and surveyed it approvingly. We were only set to play two hours, and that suited me fine. My fingers were not as tough as they used to be when I played more regularly. At one of the gigs I had to tape a couple of fingers because of developing blisters.

I tuned to Paul's keyboard, starting with the G and working downward. Paul hit the keys for me and nodded an okay as I checked all four strings. Jim tuned softly, standing close to the keyboard. He adjusted the slide on his trumpet. "Close enough for jazz," he said, repeating a musicians' quip that had been around for years.

People had begun arriving. At seven on the button, Jim counted off and we lead off with a swinging rendition of our theme: "A Foggy Day." Jim didn't use a mute, but he played softly, and Paul was great on piano, a nice light touch. Later we played the song that meant so much to me years ago, "Cheek to Cheek," which I still think of the title as "Dancing Cheek to Cheek." Has great chord changes that build upwards, giving it a nice lift. And playing it, and remembering Keely singing it, didn't make me sad, like the first few times I played it after she died. I just smiled to myself, enjoying the melody.

We got nice, polite applause, especially when Jim sang "What a Wonderful World," the tune made so popular by Louis Armstrong. Jim doesn't sound like Armstrong, but he does have a good jazz voice, slightly guttural, and his sense of rhythm and timing is impeccable. Like Armstrong, he'd get a hair behind the beat and then catch up, giving an easy, swinging feel to the lyrics.

During the two-hour job, we only took one five-minute break, and we were back at it. It was during the break that Boyd Bruton came up to me. I'd spotted him in the audience earlier. He was among several people I knew at the reception.

"Well," he said, when he approached me with his broad Santa Claus smile, "are you quitting your day job as a crime writer?"

I returned his smile. "No, sticking with that, but this is fun."

He leaned forward, his belly thrust outward, and spoke more softly. "Well, you've sure got plenty to write about here lately."

"Never any lack of subjects," I said, adding, ". . . unfortunately."

"Your buddy the SBI agent making any progress?" His voice was even softer, more conspiratorial. I could smell the alcohol on his breath. It was not unpleasant, but I straightened slightly so he wasn't so close.

"Oh, you'd have to ask him that question. All I know is that he and the sheriff and everyone are working very hard. Around the clock, I think you'd say." I was determined to get in that plug for the sheriff and others.

"Well," he said again as if he started all of his sentences with that word, "there's talk that the sheriff is not really up to the job. In fact there's a petition going around to that effect."

"Yes, I've heard that," I said, thinking to myself, and you, you sanctimonious bastard are one of those who've signed the petition. But I didn't say anything further.

Bruton bobbed his head, "Well, maybe he needs to be replaced."

I couldn't help it: "With whom?"

"I think folks could come up with someone . . . someone more experienced," he said.

I thought about Bruton's friend I met at the press conference: Russ Ricker, the tall guy with the pinched, narrow face, the one Patty Davies said had excellent crime-solving experience in Reading or Philadelphia.

I didn't say anything, just gave a noncommittal nod, and I heard Jim clear his throat and I knew we were ready to resume playing. I tried a smile at Bruton and picked up my bass, checked the tuning with a G that Paul sounded on his keyboard, bowed quick harmonics on the other three strings, and indicated to Jim I was ready.

He had called up "Satin Doll," another great tune that was fun to play, and a few measures into it I was not even thinking about Boyd Bruton and the petition.

Chapter Twenty

Friday morning I was up early. I had waked thinking about the cooking I needed to do today in preparation for having Elly, her mother, and Martin over for their first meal here at my little house. And I wanted to do it right, and impress them. I had fixed coffee and stood in the kitchen sipping a cup, planning what I needed to do first.

First I would finish my coffee and step out on the deck, see what the morning looked like. Okay, tend to Janey, check on her and speak to her, and then step out on the deck—stepping over the neck of my still-shrouded bass that lay on the living room floor. After the deck, I'd take the cover off the bass and actually stand it up in the corner on its stand. Heck, now I'd go out on the deck, but first I'd replenish my coffee cup and take that out with me.

The weather remained nice and was supposed to be mild today and tomorrow, and tomorrow was the big annual Christmas parade in downtown Manteo. Tree lighting, carols, and that sort of thing. Weather promised to cooperate. The sun was out, the sky a nice Carolina blue.

After enjoying the weather outside in the sunshine a few minutes, I went inside, picked up the bass and uncovered it, put the cover away in the closet in the second bedroom and stood the bass in the corner. I looked around the room. Later today I would vacuum a bit, dust, move my computer and crap off the dinette table and set it for the four of us tonight. Okay, lots to do, and the first thing I figured I'd better do would be to make my chocolate fudge cake and refrigerate it.

In preparation, I put the recipe a lawyer friend had given me out on the counter so I could check that over as I assembled the ingredients that would go into my chocolate fudge cake. A couple of the ingredients I needed to get to room temperature—the unsalted butter, four large eggs.

I turned my oven to preheat at 425 degrees. And I prepared my nine-inch Springform cake pan. I had no idea what a Springform pan was until I went down to the kitchen place in Nags Head the day before. The sides snap around the base, and can be removed when the cake is done. Also there I got some parchment paper, and I thought that had gone out with the monks of the Middle Ages. I lined the bottom of the pan with buttered parchment paper.

I had my one pound of semisweet chocolate chips; two tablespoons of all-purpose flour; and two teaspoons of instant espresso coffee powder. The espresso coffee powder I'd brought back from Paris in the spring.

Then I got busy, trying to clean the kitchen as I went. First I put the chocolate chips in a medium saucepan over low heat with ten tablespoons of the unsalted butter and began to let that melt together. When it was about half melted, I took it off the heat and stirred it until it was smooth, set it aside and let it cool for a few minutes.

Meanwhile, in a large mixing bowl, I began beating the eggs with an electric mixer on medium-low speed until frothy. I increased the speed to high and beat until the eggs were light in color, thick, fluffy, and almost tripled in volume. That took about five minutes. I beat in the flour and espresso coffee powder, and then stirred in roughly one-fourth of the egg mixture into the chocolate to lighten it. Next I folded in the rest of the chocolate mixture into the eggs.

And I spooned the batter into the Springform pan and

baked it for seventeen minutes. Took it out and let it cool on a rack for about ten minutes. I actually had one of these racks already on hand. Then I stuck the cake in the refrigerator, wiped my hands in satisfaction and said to Janey, "How about that?"

She said bobbed her head and said, "Shit."

"Now listen, Janey," I said, "you're going to have to clean up your language before our guests arrive."

She said, "Shit," again.

I figured that in about thirty minutes the cake would be ready to cut. If it came out as it was supposed to, it would be rather spongy and the center should be soft like a chocolate mousse. I planned to serve it chilled with a dollop of real whipped cream on top. And I'd bought the heavy cream yesterday, and made sure I had a bit of vanilla extract on hand.

All set with the dessert.

I finished cleaning up the kitchen.

Now I figured I'd prepare my World Famous Salad Dressing. Well, that might be exaggerating it. That's because I rarely made it the same way. Heck, I used to do more cooking than I'd recalled when I first asked Elly for dinner and bragged about getting the Julia Child book. Some of it was coming back to me.

I got out my ingredients for the salad dressing and started to work. In a small bowl, I put in five tablespoons of white wine vinegar, a half teaspoon of Dijon mustard, a half a teaspoon of minced shallots, one extra-large egg yolk at room temperature, three-fourths a teaspoon of kosher salt, and one-fourth a teaspoon of freshly ground black pepper. After I whisked this all together, I slowly began adding about a half a cup of extra virgin olive oil.

Voila!

I was beginning to feel like a real chef. All I needed was one of those tall white hats and a fancy apron—instead of the dishcloth I'd stuck in the waistband of my slacks.

I knew I was making the salad dressing too soon, but I'd

put it in the refrigerator and whisk it again just before putting it on the salad.

Took a break before starting the chicken and the rest of the meal. Have to set the table best I could, also. Make some sweet iced tea. A real Southern thing no matter the season.

I had to fight an urge to call Balls, see if anything had broken loose. I decided not to do it yet, so I sat at my dinette table—slash—desk, and made notes of what I knew about the investigation so far, and not just the bodies, but what was suspected as the motive—getting rid of anyone who might jeopardize the top man's operation. That had to be it. Killing the hit men in the BMW might be eliminating two who knew the top man and could finger him, or there might also be a touch of avarice . . . taking back the money and not making the final payment. Also, if Balls suspects the main guy is local, who could it possibly be. No one knows, obviously, and it certainly appears that he's taken deadly measures to make sure no one finds out.

I sat there staring out the front window; I was no nearer to an answer than when I started. Of course there was no sense in my telling myself that it wasn't my job to solve the investigation. Yet, I couldn't help it. Immersing myself in these things had become part of my nature. Maybe it always had been my obsession to solve riddles, puzzles—but it was more than that. It was a lot more than solving a mystery. It was helping put away evil, those scumbags that didn't need to be polluting the human race.

As the late Willie Boy Applewaite had said, I want to get the sonsabitches.

Now, however, I told myself is not the time to think about that. Tonight is supposed to be a festive dinner party. And I want to make it a good one. I got up and began to put away my laptop, files, and other papers that had accumulated on my dinette table. Stowed it in the second bedroom, which was becoming a catchall room. Then I set the table with a nice set of dishes and flatware I had bought when I moved in—and had almost never used. I had four chairs that more or less matched the dinette table. I picked up four large books and put them on Martin's chair, then added a fair sized red cushion on top of the books. That ought to do him. I put his chair close to where Elly would sit, her mother on the other side of Martin.

I planned to have chicken, some sautéed small red potatoes, and fresh delicate asparagus spears, also sautéed separately with a bit of olive oil. Now the chicken: I was going to prepare it in what I considered a special way. Although baked or roasted, it comes out looking and tasting like Southern fried chicken, but not at all greasy. I start with a whole chicken because I'm an expert, I figure, at cutting up a chicken. In fact, I once wrote a lighthearted newspaper feature piece about how to cut up a chicken. That was the fun part of newspaper work: You could write features about anything that struck your fancy. It didn't all have to be dastardly crimes and such.

Once the chicken was properly disassembled, and I'd dipped it in a bit of milk to get it good and moist, I would put the pieces in a paper bag that contained flour, salt and pepper, shake it good to give a nice coating. To cook it, I'd preheat the oven to 400 degrees and place the chicken in an iron skillet (one I'd had for years, passed down to me by my parents) with just a touch of olive oil in the bottom and a couple or three pats of butter on the chicken, which would be arranged lying flat in the skillet. I never really time how long it took to cook—twenty or thirty minutes maybe—but I keep checking it and when it looks good and done, it is. I even put the floured gizzard in there too. Figured I'd sneak that out and eat it before Elly, her mother, and Martin arrived.

By five o'clock that afternoon I was ready to begin the serious business of actually cooking. Everything, including the salads, was ready to begin. I even had a pan of dinner rolls ready to be baked. Now, if I could just time everything right so that part of the dinner didn't get cold while I cooked the rest.

It should be fun and I was looking forward to it. But I wasn't sure I wanted to do this often. Lot of work. In a way, though, it had surely mostly kept me from thinking about murder and mayhem.

Right at six o'clock, I saw Elly's Pontiac pull into my cul-de-sac. I wiped my hands on the still present dishcloth and went out on the deck to call out a greeting. Elly carried a dish of something. She looked great as always; she had pinned her hair back and I liked that because it showed off her face and neck. Little Martin was dressed with what looked like a new shirt and his hair was combed so it didn't stick up very much in the back. Mrs. Pedersen, standing tall and erect, smiled as she surveyed my house, and nodded approvingly.

They came up the outside stairs and I ushered them in with a flourish. I took their coats and jackets to put on the bed in that second bedroom, and all the while Mrs. Pedersen continued surveying, and saying how nice everything looked. Elly added, "And supper smells wonderful, Harrison." Then she handed me the plate. "Mother wanted to bake you some chocolate chip cookies because she knows how much you like them. Extra chocolate chips in them too."

I thanked Mrs. Pedersen and set the cookies on the counter. "They won't last long," I said.

Martin went straight to Janey's cage and said, "Oh, boy, a bird." He glanced at Elly. "A parrot?"

"No," I said, "it's a parakeet, Martin. Smaller than a parrot."

"Does he talk?" Martin asked, his concentration remaining on Janey, who eyed him warily.

"It's a little girl bird, Martin. Her name is Janey." Then I said, "Girl parakeets are not the ones that talk."

Elly gave me a look. She'd heard Janey's vocabulary before.

Then Elly asked if there was something she could help

me with. I suggested they try some of the cheese and crackers I'd set out in a plate on the counter. "Oh," I said, "if you don't mind getting iced tea out. That would help. Everything is about ready. Chicken's almost done, rolls, too, and I'm just finishing up the potatoes and asparagus." I glanced at Martin, who was still studying Janey. "I just know Martin is crazy about asparagus." He turned and eyed me, went back to Janey. She stayed as far from him as she could in the confines of her cage.

Elly went straight to the cabinet to get glasses for the iced tea. The fact that Elly knew exactly where the glasses were wasn't lost on Mrs. Pedersen.

I finished sautéing the potatoes and the asparagus in a separate pan. There was just a hint of fresh garlic in the asparagus. Not enough to disturb the neighbors.

I brought the rolls and chicken out and Mrs. Pedersen and Elly marveled. "Looks exactly like fried chicken," Mrs. Pedersen said.

"I think you'll find it tastes like fried chicken, too," I said. "Only not at all greasy."

Shortly we sat down to eat and I must say that I was proud of the meal. Elly and I opted for the dark meat, the thighs and legs; Mrs. Pedersen got a breast and we cut a small piece of breast for Martin. He also said he wanted a little drumstick, so I broke apart the wings and gave him two "little drumsticks."

The salad was well received, also, and Elly and her mother both complimented me on my World Famous Dressing. With a great deal of encouragement, Elly got Martin to eat the smallest of the asparagus spears.

When we had finished with the chicken and the rest of the meal (Martin actually ate two tiny pieces of asparagus), Elly helped me clear the table for dessert. Proudly, I brought out my chocolate fudge cake and the bowl of whipped cream, which had turned out perfectly. The cake was even better than I'd thought it would be. I beamed in satisfaction and glowed in the compliments.

We all leaned back from my little dinette table. "Coffee, anyone?" I asked.

They declined.

But Elly said, "You have some, Harrison, if you'd like. And maybe your cigar?"

"I'll wait on the cigar," I said.

Elly and her mother insisted on helping me with the clean up. I do have a dishwasher that hardly ever gets used, but we loaded it completely and turned it on. We sat in the living room for a few minutes and they both said how impressed they were with the meal. I grinned and was happy, too. Martin had left Janey and gone to my bass. He stood there looking at it.

"Want to hear what it sounds like, Martin?" I asked.

He nodded and I went to it and plucked a few notes. He put his hand on his stomach. "I can feel it," he said, a smile on his face.

Then the phone rang. "Excuse me," I said, and I answered it. "Yes, Balls, what's up?"

"You got your sweetie or someone there with you?"

"Yes, Elly and her mother and son just had dinner with me. You know, a private dinner with Chef Weav."

"Could tell by the way you answered," he said. "Won't bother you while you're courting and trying to influence your future mother-in-law but wanted to let you know I've been poking more into that petition those clowns are circulating. Looks like your friend Patty Davies is the one behind it, and they're pushing this guy Ricker to replace the sheriff."

"Not going to happen, is it?" I ignored the business about Patty Davies being my friend.

"Of course it's not going to happen. I've met this Ricker, and . . ." His voice trailed off.

"And what?"

"He's . . . he's uncomfortable about something. Don't know what yet, but uncomfortable."

"You still in Manteo?"

"Practically live here now, Lorraine thinks."

"See you there tomorrow?"

"Yeah, big Christmas parade day. Want to keep an eye on things then, maybe talk again with your friend Patty."

I didn't let it pass this time. "Not my friend, Balls."

He chuckled. "Get back to your sweetie . . . and future mother-in-law."

I apologized to Elly and Mrs. Pedersen for the phone call.

"No need to apologize, Harrison," Elly said. Then she got that sly smile: "I'm sure Agent Twiddy needed to check with you to see how your investigation was progressing."

I raised an eyebrow at her but didn't respond.

She shrugged, and kept that smile. Mildly taunting me.

With a perplexed expression, Mrs. Pedersen said, "I think your parakeet just said something. Plain as it could be." She tilted her head, a twinkle in her eyes. "And not a very nice word, either."

Elly spoke up. "Female parakeets don't talk."

"This one did," Mrs. Pedersen said, and gave a little laugh.

Shortly after that, it was time for them to go home. "Work day for me tomorrow at the Christmas Shop," Elly said, "and Martin needs to think about bedtime."

He gave a groan.

Once again they were very complimentary about the meal and Elly said that I'd convinced her that I was, indeed, a gourmet cook. She said, "I take back what I've been saying about those boring ham sandwiches you are always fixing yourself. I know now you can actually do much, much better."

As I retrieved their coats, I said, "Parade tomorrow and Christmas tree lighting?"

Mrs. Pedersen said, "I'm taking Martin to see the parade and see Santa Claus, and maybe stay for the tree lighting on the waterfront."

"I'm going too," I said.

Elly studied me. "I suppose Agent Twiddy will be there also?"

I nodded.

"Please be careful," she said. "I have a feeling . . . a feeling that . . . I don't know." She shook her head.

I tried briefly and rather lamely to put her at ease. But the truth was I had a feeling, also—that damp and heavy sensation in your chest or the pit of your stomach, a sense that something bad could happen.

Chapter Twenty-One

In contrast to a forecast for mild weather, Saturday dawned chilly and cloudy, with a brisk northeast wind. After all, it was December and weather suitable, I supposed, for a Christmas parade and Santa Claus. In addition to the parade, several musical events were scheduled, most of them right on the courthouse steps. At the pavilion stage at the end of the block from the courthouse, the band Old Enough to Know Better would perform. I knew I had to take them in. They were very good, and the electric bass player was excellent.

One of my all-time favorite groups, Molasses Creek from Ocracoke Island, would be performing that weekend in Hatteras. I was sorry they wouldn't be in Manteo also. Earlier, before the killings and ensuing investigation, I'd thought about going down to Hatteras to attend their performance. Wasn't leaving this area now.

The tree lighting, of course, wouldn't be until about six o'clock. Two or three choral groups were to perform during the day, and there'd be a sing-along of Christmas carols. Okay, maybe quaint, small-town stuff, but comforting to know that it still went on. I was happy about it.

I planned to spend most of the day in Manteo. My first stop, before the festivities got underway, would be to check in at the sheriff's office, see if I could catch up with Balls.

And I did. I went upstairs to one of the interview rooms and found Balls, sitting alone, looking dejected, a yellow pad with notes on it spread out in front of him.

He made a sort of grunting sound when I tapped on the door and stepped inside. He was behind a metal table, slumped back in a chair. He had his forearms stretched out before him, toying with a ballpoint pen. He wore his rumpled tan sport coat, but a heavier windbreaker hung on the back of a chair near the wall. He shook his head wearily.

I sat in the straight back metal chair on the other side of the table. "Not much luck, huh?" I said.

He twisted his mouth and shook his head one more time.

I didn't say anything.

He slid one sheet across the table to me. It was the petition, maybe a newer one. I glanced at it. Patty Davies' name was again at the top. There were probably twenty-five or more names scrawled on the sheet, with a notation at the bottom that said "more." He puffed out a sigh of air. "Linda Shackleford from *The Coastland Times* called me earlier today, said Patty Davies was coming to the office to deliver another petition." He inclined his head toward the sheet I held. "That one," he said. "Didn't have anything else going on so I just happened to go down Budleigh Street to the paper and was there when Patty Davies came in."

"Oh?" I said.

"Asked her who they were pushing to replace Sheriff Albright. She hemmed-and-hawed a bit and then said they thought that Ricker guy would be a good candidate."

"What does he say? You been in touch with him?"

"Not really interested in him yet, Weav. Oh, I'll get to him eventually, but what I really wanted to know from Ms. Davies is who is behind this push to get the sheriff out." He made that dismissive face. "She claims it's a 'groundswell of opinion' that's behind it. Those are her words. Groundswell of opinion. That's bullshit, of course. It comes from up there in Southern Shores or Martin's Point."

I wanted to be careful how I said it, but I couldn't help but wonder what in the hell this had to do with the ongoing investigation of the multiple killings. Okay, so they weren't happy with the sheriff and wanted someone else with what they considered more proven law enforcement experience or success. I squirmed a bit in my chair as if trying to get comfortable. I didn't meet Balls' gaze.

But I think he read my thoughts.

He leaned forward in his chair. "I've said all along that the guy behind all of this is local. Now suppose—just suppose—and I know it's a long stretch but suppose this head guy wants his own man in the county heading law enforcement? Be easier for him."

I must have made something of a face.

"Okay, okay. It's a stretch, I know. But just suppose . . ." He let his voice fade. He knew and I knew it was a straw he clutched at because there just wasn't anything else.

But I picked up the thread he'd left dangling: "The person they may be pushing is this fellow Ricker, Russ Ricker. He was at the press conference." I shrugged. "Come on, Balls, he's just visiting here, apparently with Boyd Bruton." I thought about the connection and gave a short, mocking laugh. "Santa Claus? Really?"

"I know, I know," Balls said, the weariness coming back into his voice and his posture as he slumped back in his chair.

I changed the subject. "You going to the parade and all the other festivities?"

He gave a lopsided smile. "Sort of make my presence known?"

"Well, might be fun."

"I'll probably mosey around there later." He gave a short chuckle. "Right now I think I'll just brood. Yeah, brood. Isn't that a word you writers use?"

"Do it all the time, Balls." I stood. "Well, I'm going to go down there, see what's happening. Listen to some of the music."

Just then Balls' cell phone, which lay on the desk in front of him, chirped. He answered. "Yeah. Let him in." He disconnected. To me he said, "I gotta talk to someone."

"Okay," I said. "Then you can go back to brooding."

He nodded, but looked at his phone as if willing it to ring again. "Lab guys will be calling back I hope."

As I stepped out of the office Balls was using and started to turn left, a solidly built man with a full reddish beard came from the other direction. He wore dirty jeans, a greasy windbreaker, and a faded baseball cap, his unkempt long hair sticking out from the edges of the cap. He had come up the back stairs, and I was sure he was the one Balls had instructed on the phone to be let in. The man eyed me with a blank, noncommittal expression and strode into the office with Balls. He shut the door behind him.

I turned and continued on my way downstairs. I got a smile on my face. Balls had said I'd probably seen one or more of the DEA agents on the case. That was one of them. Undercover, obviously. He looked the part. That's the reason he wanted to come in the back way, not be seen as being friendly with anyone in the sheriff's office.

At the top of the stairs I met Sheriff Albright coming up. His long-time assistant Mabel trudged beside him. He was taking his time, in deference I'm sure, to Mabel, who puffed and wheezed, grimacing with each step on swollen ankles. She'd finally given up on trying various diets. She has a kindly face and I like her.

I spoke to both of them. Sheriff Albright managed to smile briefly, but I knew it was an effort for him with everything that was going on. I continued downstairs and out a side door that opened onto Sir Walter Raleigh Street. Didn't want to interrupt any performance that was probably taking place on the courthouse's front porch.

Crowds had begun to form along the sidewalks and in front of the courthouse. A trio consisting of two guitars and a mandolin had just finished performing on the porch. A smattering of applause greeted their bows as they stepped away. From the distance, I heard music from one of the high school bands. The parade would be coming up this way shortly.

Then I saw Patty Davies talking animatedly to a couple I didn't know. As usual, she leaned into her audience. She was short but came across so energetically that it was easy to forget how small she was. I couldn't hear what she was saying but the shifting mobility of her face signaled that it was important to her, urgent, as most things were.

I sidled over and spoke to her, only a slight interruption in what she was saying to the man and woman she addressed. She acknowledged me and essentially signed off with the couple; they smiled briefly and made what I considered a quick getaway.

"How's the petition going?" I asked, glancing around at the crowd as if I were simply making idle conversation.

"Oh, we're getting names. Getting names. You better believe it." She put her hand on my arm and leaned into me. "People are fed up. Fed up with all this violence. Terrible violence. We need someone who can bring strict law enforcement to the county."

"Who you got in mind, Patty?"

"The who is not as important as getting someone who can take charge. End this violence."

"This fellow Ricker?"

She paused a moment. I saw some of the intensity drain from her face. "He's a possibility, of course." Then she regained her momentum. "A real possibility." She vigorously nodded her head. "Fact is, we need a person who is proven in law enforcement work."

"Sheriff Albright is surely experienced and he's got the SBI backing him up and—"

She broke in with, "Sheriff Albright's a good man. A nice man. We don't need just a nice man, however, we need

. . . well, you know what we need. You're experienced in writing about this stuff. You know how important it is to have really top quality people leading an investigation." She took a breath.

I used that pause to interject what I wanted to know: "Who's behind this movement, Patty? I know you're deeply involved, but who started it? Did you?"

From her expression, I could tell she mentally went back to her script. "No I didn't start it. It's a groundswell of opinion."

Uh-huh, I thought. Same thing she told Balls.

She spotted someone else in the crowd she needed to buttonhole. "Good to see you," she said. As she turned to scurry off, she said, "I know you're friendly with the sheriff and his staff, but you really ought to think about signing the petition that's circulating." She waved a rolled up sheet of paper she clutched in her right hand.

I nodded. "Take it under advisement," I said, but she was already gone.

The marching band music was getting closer, and the people along the curb melded together in a more solid line. Young parents made sure their children were in front of them so the little ones could have unobstructed view of the parade—and Santa Claus.

It was then that I saw Russ Ricker standing off to my left. I had the feeling he'd been watching my exchange with Patty. There was something about him, maybe his stance or the aura of aloneness that surrounded him, that made him look out of place at a Christmas parade. I don't know what it was, but it was a strong feeling that I got.

He was watching me, as I was him. I couldn't tell whether he might turn and walk away if I approached him. As if he might flee. But I took a chance on it and inched my way toward him, mouthing apologies to a few of the parents that I edged past. He didn't flee, but watched me approach.

He stood there, tall and gaunt, the collar of his windbreaker turned up, but it didn't appear warm. With his shoulders raised high toward his neck and his head thrust forward, he looked something like a question mark. I went close and gave a weak smile. "Mr. Ricker," I said. "Don't know whether you remember me. I met you at the press conference. I'm—"

"I know who you are," he said. He glanced around as if he thought someone might be approaching us.

I figured I'd dive right in, and I tried another smile I guess to soften what I was about to say: "I understand you might be a candidate for sheriff?" Couched it more as what I hoped would sound like a friendly question.

"Oh, no," he said. "Oh, no," and he shook his head vigorously. He cast his eyes around at the crowd.

"Well, with that petition and all—"

Again he interrupted me, but he trained his stare at my face, as he said, "Your friend, Agent Twiddy. I was looking for him." He shivered as if he might be cold. Or was it nervousness? I wasn't sure.

I was mildly surprised he knew Balls was my friend. "He was in the courthouse a short while ago. Sheriff's office. I just saw him."

"He's not there now. I was up there."

I glanced around. "He's probably out here somewhere, getting ready to watch the parade."

The marching band music got closer, and the first of the parade came into view. Six drum majorettes in sparkling costumes strutted in front of the Manteo High School band.

I raised my voice. "Can I help you with anything, Mr. Ricker?"

He jerkily shook his head again but he wouldn't look at me.

The band passed us by. Then there were fire trucks and Dare County emergency vehicles, the drivers and volunteers hanging on the sides and waving at the viewers, tossing out cellophane wrapped miniature candy canes to the youngsters who scampered to gather them.

I was at something of a loss as to what to say to Ricker next. I didn't want him to slip away. But he kept darting his eyes right and left, apparently hoping to spot Balls. Curiosity gnawed at me. Why was he so nervous? Something was surely eating at him. Lamely I said, "I'm sure we'll run into Agent Twiddy around here somewhere."

Ricker didn't respond to me. He stared at the parade, his eyes wide, then up and down the street again. Here came the First Flight High School marching band and right behind it was a float with Santa Claus—Boyd Bruton—sitting upon a throne, and also tossing candy canes out to the children. Bruton was in full Santa Claus regalia, red suit and flowing white beard. He didn't have to pad his stomach. It was there prominently.

It was then that the most curious thing happened.

Ricker looked terrified. It was an almost palatable expression upon his face, around his eyes. And Santa Claus stared at him, and threw candy at him. I don't mean tossed candy. He threw it like a missile. Two or three pieces of candy hit Ricker in the chest. He stood frozen, but a look of defiance in the set of his jaw. His hands fisted tightly by his sides.

Boyd Bruton's eyes narrowed even more than normally as he stared at Ricker. Then Bruton did something that etched in my mind. He held his right hand forward, index finger pointing, thumb raised. Like a pistol. Pointing at Ricker. Then just as quickly Bruton went back to being Santa Claus, the ho, ho, ho bit, and smiling and tossing candy to the kids.

Santa Claus's float passed on by and young children applauded and called out greetings to Santa.

I turned my head. Ricker was gone. Disappeared.

Chapter Twenty-Two

With my brief encounter with Ricker, I was convinced he was transformed from the man I'd first seen, the one who was contained and seemed to be in complete control. He was now a man shaken. A man terrified.

Of Santa Claus? Of Boyd Bruton?

Then, suddenly, like a fist to my stomach, I knew something, too. That wasn't Santa Claus, that was a killer masquerading. My mind began clicking at warp speed. Boyd Bruton was one of those behind the petition, and Ricker had been his guest, being pushed for sheriff, and now he obviously wasn't seeking the job, and Ricker was terribly afraid, afraid of the man who lived in Southern Shores—near where Willie Boy was murdered, and close to The Marketplace where the two hit men were surprised and killed. Was Ricker one of the loose ends to tie up? Maybe I was making a wild leap of assumptions, but I'd had those sudden feelings before, a knowledge, an awareness that came in a flash. And I'd always been right to heed it.

Then, looking around, I spotted Ricker again, well back from the crowd, almost shrinking into a doorway at one of the shops. I pushed my way through the crowd, mumbling apologies as I bumped shoulders and squeezed past spectators and their children.

I stepped up to the doorway and stood in front of Ricker.

"We've got to find Agent Twiddy. You need to talk to him."

Ricker nodded his thin, drawn face, his arms pressed to his sides like he was trying to hide, withdraw into himself.

I looked around the crowd, trying to spot Balls. I didn't see him. I tried his cell and it went straight to voice mail. Far to my right I caught a quick glimpse of Mrs. Pedersen. She was leaning forward, holding Martin's hand, and saying something to him. Were it not for the urgency I felt, I would have gone to greet them. Putting my hand on Ricker's arm I said, "We'll go find Agent Twiddy."

Ricker shook his head. "I've got to go," he said, his voice uneven, trembling.

"We can find him," I said, and moved through the crowd again to step off the curb and peer up the street toward the courthouse and beyond. "He's bound to be up . . ." and I turned back and Ricker was gone—again.

He had vanished. I stepped back on the curb and craned my neck to my left. One of the parents frowned at me as I tried to maneuver for better sight. I brushed against the man's little boy, and the man said to me, "Watch it there, fellow."

"Sorry," I said and pushed my way back through the crowd.

Ricker was nowhere to be seen. There were hordes of people watching the parade, which was winding down now; the last float went by. But the people remained, milling about. Music started from somewhere. It was a Christmas carol being performed by a group of adults on the steps of the courthouse. The days were so much shorter and darkness would be coming on soon.

I couldn't find Ricker. And I didn't see Balls. Back toward the courthouse I did see young Deputy Dorsey. Jaywalking across the street, I hurried to Dorsey and got his attention.

"Merry Christmas," he said, a big grin on his ruddy face, made even more flushed by the chilling wind.

"You seen Agent Twiddy?" I leaned into him, urgency in my voice.

"Yes sir, a little while ago. Back over there." He pointed to Budleigh Street. I nodded a thanks. With quick steps I turned the corner onto Budleigh. The crowds were thinner there. I looked up and down the street. Didn't see Balls. And I didn't see Ricker either.

The parade had completely ended. High school band members in uniform milled around with the crowd. Some of them carried their instruments.

I moved back to the front of the courthouse and scanned the crowd in vain. The choral group had left the porch. In a few minutes, I knew another musical group would probably take over. But in the lull, and behind me, I heard a familiar voice.

"Looking for someone?"

It was Chief Deputy Odell Wright, standing tall beside me and looking every inch the professional in his uniform, complete today with tie and sheriff department jacket. He had a half-smile on his coffee-colored face. His silver name-tag says "O. Wright," and he has often wryly remarked that he is one of the original Wright Brothers. Usually the person he's directing this deadpan delivery to doesn't know what to say in return.

"Trying to find Balls, Agent Twiddy," I said, casting my eyes around at the people.

"Haven't seen him," Wright said. He caught the tone of my voice. "What's up?"

"That fellow Ricker, Russ Ricker needs to talk to him." I didn't know how much of my own unsubstantiated suspicion I should relay.

Wright eyed me. He knew there was more.

"I think he has some suspicions," I said. Then I added, "And Ricker seems very, very nervous."

Wright's eyes narrowed. "Uh-oh," he said. "That doesn't sound good."

I kept my vigilance going, looking for Balls in the crowd.

Wright didn't want to let it go. "He must have someone in mind?" It was more of a question than a statement.

I didn't want to say. What? Santa Claus? Jeeze, that would sound a little screwy. "I believe he might," I said.

With a nod, the deputy acknowledged that that was all I was going to say at the moment. "I'll see if I can find him." He pulled his cell phone from his belt, scrolled a bit, and punched in a preset number. "See if he'll answer," Wright said. After several rings, Wright shook his head, and left a brief message to Balls that we were in front of the courthouse and looking for him. Needed to talk with him.

The chairman of the county commissioners took over the microphone on the courthouse porch. He welcomed everyone and announced that in a few minutes they would have the lighting of "a traditional holiday tree."

Hmm, I thought. Not a Christmas tree? Really? Oh, well, I'd save my rants against political correctness for another day.

Questions nagged at my subconscious. What was it that occasioned the fear, the nervousness in Ricker? What was it he had discovered, or believed he discovered? Why all of a sudden? And that expression on Boyd Bruton's face, which the Santa Claus costume couldn't conceal. It was a deadly anger. Directed at Ricker. It may have been an imaginary pistol he "fired" with index finger and thumb, but the message was real. A killer message.

Just then, Wright's cell phone chirped. He answered. "Yes sir, Agent Twiddy. Mr. Weaver is here and wants to talk with you. Yes sir, at the courthouse. It's about that fellow Ricker. I understand. We'll see you then, and . . ." But apparently Balls had signed off.

Wright turned to me, a wry smile playing around his lips. "Hard to hold onto Agent Twiddy. He said he'd be at the courthouse in about thirty minutes and for you to go there and wait for him. Didn't say where he was, but knowing Agent Twiddy there's no telling except that he's hot on the trail of something." Wright shook his head, probably with a feeling of admiration for Balls plus a touch of amusement at Balls' bang-up, full-speed-ahead approach to investigations.

I couldn't spot Ricker anywhere, so figured I might as well cool my heels up in the sheriff's office until Balls got there.

Trudging upstairs to the sheriff's offices, I was in for a surprise. Young Deputy Dorsey met me in the hallway. His face remained flushed from the cold outside. "There's someone in the interview room waiting for you or Agent Twiddy."

It was Russ Ricker. He stood behind the table, eyes wide and shoulders still pulled up like he was cold. I sensed that he had been pacing back in forth in the small room, but he stopped and stared at me when I entered.

"Let's sit down," I said to him, and he bobbed his head like his neck and head weren't connected.

We both sat for a moment in the straight back metal chairs. I kept my eyes on him. He licked his thin lips but it didn't appear to do much good.

"Agent Twiddy will be here shortly," I said.

He glanced down at his hands, clenched together in his lap.

"Are you in danger, Mr. Ricker?"

He almost jumped; his head came up, staring at me, his eyes wide. He nodded and said, "I think so. Yes, I think so." His voice was surprisingly even, in contrast to his trembling frame. "Yes."

"Can we talk a little while we wait for Agent Twiddy?

"I guess." Then, "You're his friend, aren't you?"

"Of Agent Twiddy, yes."

He nodded again.

I wanted to try to get him calmed down a level or two. "You're safe here in the sheriff's office," I said. I knew it was something of a venture, but maybe it would open him up a bit.

"I figured," he said. "Reason I came." His mouth twisted in a wry, self-deprecating way. "I'm an experienced former cop. Not used to seeking refuge."

Watching him, I continued to have that feeling of disconnect between the seasoned lawman I'd first seen at the press conference and this man sitting before me. Okay, I thought, I'd jab at him again:

"It's Boyd Bruton, isn't it?"

At the name, Ricker's body went more rigid, as if either ready for flight or fight. Then the air went out of his chest with an audible sigh and his shoulders slumped. "Yes," he said, his head nodding again in emphasis.

Then he got an expression on his lean face as if he were puzzled. "He's different. So different," Ricker said. He stared at me as if he wanted me to understand. "I've known him for years. Back in Reading. He was different. He made all that money, you know, with that software he developed for banks and businesses. But it didn't seem like the money was enough."

Ricker twisted his hands together. "He moved down here, and it was after that he was different. I didn't have that much contact with him when he moved down here but he stayed in touch and I came down here a couple of times, and then he started talking about wanting me to be the sheriff here." He twisted in his chair and rolled his shoulders, loosening them. "I think he wanted to run things." He shook his head and said again, "He was different."

He leaned forward as if he were suddenly going to confide in me. "I think he started using drugs. He would be fine for a while and then get mad or think people were out to get him. He was getting really paranoid."

He was silent, and I was too. I could hear muffled conversations out in the hallway, but we were being left alone. There was no window in the little interrogation room but I knew it was fully dark outside.

"You're still friends with him. Something happen to-day?"

I saw the changed expression; fear returned.

"What happened today?" I pressed.

He ducked his head in thought, and then turned his gaze toward me, staring hard. "I came over from Hilton Garden where I'm staying to help him get ready as Santa Claus." He licked at his lips again. "I'd thought he'd been acting funny lately . . ."

"Funny?"

"You know, like he had other things on his mind. He was distracted, sort of out of it, and he looked like he hadn't been sleeping much." He stopped and I wasn't sure he was going to continue. But I waited him out. "He disappeared a couple of times."

I started to ask him what he meant by "disappeared," but decided to see if he would continue. And he did. He said, "Like the night those two guys were killed."

I wanted to ask him how he knew Bruton disappeared that night but I figured it would be best to let him play it all out verbally, go back later if there were more questions. Too, I knew that Balls would be here shortly and he would do a thorough interrogation, but while he was talking I was certainly going to take advantage of it.

Ricker continued: "And the way he was acting, it was obvious he was doing drugs. I've seen enough of that in law enforcement to know it when I see it."

I nodded. "And you went over to his place today to help him get ready to play Santa Claus?"

"Yeah." He stared at his hands in his lap. He appeared to be thinking what to say next. He raised his head. "He told me to go in his closet and get his makeup bag. You know, with the beard and rouge and stuff he puts on his face. It was a big closet. I went in there and there was this bag pushed back to one side. Practically hidden. I thought it was the one he was talking about and I looked inside to make sure." He took a deep breath. "It was full of money. Must have been more than a hundred thousand dollars in there. There were bundles of one hundred dollar bills."

I thought about the third bag the motel clerk had told Balls about and how there were only two bags in the trunk of the BMW.

Ricker said, "I didn't say anything when I came out of the closet with his makeup bag. But he looked at me. Maybe I had a funny expression on my face or something." I could see Ricker's bony chest moving up and down as he breathed. "That's when I think he knew . . . and that's when I could tell he got really cold toward me, like I was the enemy. All the way over here to Manteo I drove his car and he didn't say anything, but I could tell he kept looking at me from time to time, and I was sweating."

There was a discrete tap on the door. I said, "Yes?"

Deputy Wright opened the door. "Can I speak to you?" He said it softly, but there was urgency in his voice.

I told Ricker I would just be a moment, and I stepped into the hallway.

"Agent Twiddy is on his way," Wright said, "and he says the lab guys have come through once again. He sounded real upbeat."

I raised my eyebrows. "And?"

Wright leaned in close. "He wanted to know where Boyd Bruton was."

Uh-oh, I thought. The partial palm print. That was the only thing the lab was working on as far as I knew.

Then it occurred to me, and I felt sick. It was like I'd received the blow of a fist in my stomach. I tried to swallow and my mouth suddenly felt dry. I could feel my heart beating faster. The tree lighting had occurred, and I knew that Bruton, as Santa Claus, was scheduled to appear at the Christmas Shop. I wanted to be there. Elly was there.

And Boyd Bruton would be there too.

Chapter Twenty-Three

I wanted to move quickly. Inclining my head toward the interrogation room, I ushered Deputy Wright in with me. Ricker jerked his face toward us. The fear in his face faded a bit. "Mr. Ricker," I said, "I've got to go to the Christmas Shop but Deputy Wright is going to stay with you until Agent Twiddy arrives. And he should be here in a few minutes."

Ricker moved as though he might stand, that flee or fight tensing of his body.

"You'll be fine," I said. "Just stay here."

He jerked his head up and down.

Deputy Wright moved in. He extended his hand and Ricker gave a limp handshake. Wright took the seat I had vacated. He unzipped his jacket and slipped it off, draping it on the back of his chair. Ricker had kept his windbreaker tight around his body as if he remained cold.

Nodding to them both, I turned and was gone.

I raced down the stairs, and out the side door, looped around back of the courthouse and jogged down Sir Walter Raleigh Street for a block and a half to my car.

Another driver honked at me as I pulled away from the curb, backed up, twisted the wheel and swung around forward in the opposite direction, toward Highway 64 and the short distance to the Christmas Shop. I squeezed into a left turn into the Christmas Shop's parking lot. There were only four or five cars in the lot. Most people were still at the festivities near the Manteo Waterfront. I more or less made a parking place close to the front door and bounded out of my car and up the ramp to the front door.

I wanted to hurry but made myself slow down as I entered the shop with its familiar Christmas scents and soft music. I nodded to one of the women behind the counter to my right. I glanced to my left and caught a glimpse of Santa Claus bent over speaking to a little girl. I'm not sure whether Boyd Bruton saw me or not.

I headed straight back toward the end of that hallway toward the jewelry room. I met Tina as she came out of the jewelry room and headed toward the counter in the front of the shop. She smiled and spoke and then she looked at my face, her own face mirroring the concern that must have been deeply lined on mine.

Elly was behind the counter and she gave me a big smile. Then her smile faded as she saw my expression.

"Harrison?" she said, her tone laced with concern.

"I want you to leave," I said, putting my hands on the counter and leaning close toward her.

"What do you mean? What's wrong?" I could tell her mind did a quick maternal click. "Martin? Is he okay?"

"Yes, yes," I said. "It's nothing at home. I just don't want you in here."

An announcement came over the shop's PA system that the shop was closing. It was Richard's voice. He controlled the PA system and the music that was piped in.

Elly looked puzzled. She glanced at her tiny wristwatch. "What's going on?"

I figured either Balls or Deputy Wright had called the Christmas Shop and urged the early closing.

"There could be trouble," I said. "I don't want you here. Please get your things and leave."

Elly didn't move. She just stared at me, two little vertical wrinkles between her eyebrows. "What trouble? What kind of trouble? I can't just walk out."

"Yes you can," I said. I cast a quick furtive glance over my shoulder and back to Elly. "It's Boyd Bruton. Santa Claus."

Four customers walked past the jewelry room, expressing bewilderment at the sudden closing. Richard's voice came over the PA system again, saying the shop was now closed and to please proceed to checkout.

Elly's voice registered incredulity: "Santa Claus? Mr. Bruton? What in the world . . ." Then the urgency of my demeanor fully registered. The dots got connected that second—the store closing, my sudden appearance, the need to get out of there. "Oh, my God," she said. "It can't be."

"Yes," I said. "Please get out of here—now."

"What about you?"

"Right behind you," I lied. I wasn't about to leave, not yet.

She came from behind the counter. But she didn't move quickly enough.

A figure had appeared in the passageway to the jewelry room.

A portly figure in a red suit.

Boyd Bruton had removed his wooly beard. He had hooked one side of it to the top edge of his Santa suit. The beard hung at an angle, like someone had whacked it off. His Santa hat was rolled and stuck partly into one of his baggy side pockets. His small eyes squinted at me.

"Just leaving, Mr. Bruton," I said, trying my best to sound casual, matter of fact.

"No you're not," he said. He held his head to one side and he breathed heavily.

I took Elly's arm and strolled past him out into the hallway. He took a step or two back so that he effectively blocked our passage toward the front of the store. I shrugged and turned around with Elly, our backs to Bruton, and went a few steps in the opposite direction, toward the hallway that came down from the art gallery; in front of us the floor of the store slanted down toward what years ago had been the front entrance to the shop. To our left, the hallway slanted upwards toward more galleries and the candy shop. There were different halls and rooms either way, and I thought that perhaps we could scamper away quickly enough evade Bruton.

But I sensed that Bruton had made another movement slightly to his left, creating an advantage for him no matter which way we might try to run. Then his voice was clear and cold as he said, "You were talking to Ricker. I saw that. He's running his mouth probably. Thinking wild thoughts."

I turned back to Bruton. "Maybe not so wild, Boyd." I could feel the tenseness in Elly's body as I held her arm and at the same time tried to move her behind me. I wasn't successful. She stayed close to my side, pressed against my shoulder, her breathing coming fast. My chest heaved with my breaths also, but I attempted to control my breathing, make it more normal so that my voice would be even and calm, totally and absolutely contrary to how I felt. I tried breathing in through my nose and out through my mouth.

Bruton squinted the mean, tiny eyes at me, his jaw thrust forward. "You don't think you're going anywhere do you? You think I'm going to ignore things that you've been hearing from Ricker, who turned against me after all I was trying to do for him? Huh? You think I can just ignore all of that?" His voice was rising. "I'm not going to let people walk all over me, turn against me."

"We're leaving, Boyd. Time for us to go," I said. To me my voice didn't sound like mine. There was a breathlessness in my tone.

He stepped forward. "No, you're not." From the folds of his Santa pants he pulled out a pistol. It looked like a Glock 9mm. He aimed it at my chest.

I felt Elly press harder against me, her body trembling.

"Now look, Boyd," I said, trying to stall for time.

"There's no place for you to go now. It's all over . . ." I had to raise my voice because suddenly the Christmas music got louder, then louder still. Richard had turned the volume up full blast. The Christmas song *The Little Drummer Boy* boomed louder and louder. Bruton cast his eyes up toward the speaker in the ceiling, scowling, as if annoyed with the music.

I wanted to keep him talking; as long as he talked, I knew we were relatively safe. "You're behind those killings, Boyd. The SBI and others know that now." I hoped that this was true. "You might as well put down that gun. The officers will be here right away." I surely hoped so.

Bruton said, "You don't understand anything, do you? I'm a businessman, and you've got to maintain control if you're going to stay in business."

"You're not a businessman, Boyd. You're a drug dealer. That business about developing software was probably phony—just like you being Santa Claus. A phony. You're a drug dealer."

He lifted his chin. "I'm a businessman," he said, a defiance in his tone.

"You eliminated those who threatened you in some way, Boyd," I said, utilizing a force of will I kept my voice sounding almost normal. Elly's grip was so tight on my arm the tips of her fingers dug into my flesh. I tried to control my breathing, my heart pounding in my chest, but I did everything I could to appear calm and rational.

Bruton got a sardonic half-smile on his fleshy lips. "Of course," he said. "Sometimes a businessman has to take steps to eliminate competition . . . or to keep others in line."

"Yes, and that's why you had Tom Applewaite, and then his brother, killed, or killed him yourself, and that poor young man on the causeway." I frowned at Bruton, shook my head as if in disbelief. "You even killed your own hit men."

"Shut up," Bruton snarled. His whole demeanor

changed. A dangerous rage built quickly. I could see his body tense. He lowered his head slightly, his eyes squinting at me. Slowly he began extending his arm that held the pistol. His breathing was more rapid.

The piped in music got even louder.

And just then out of the corner of my eye, I saw Eddie Greene in his motorized scooter chair, poised at the top of the gently slanting ramp to my right. I inched a little to my left so that Bruton tracked me with a slight turn of his body. This made his back turned more toward Eddie Greene. I knew Greene could see what was going on—that Boyd Bruton had Elly and me in the sights of his handgun. Bruton glanced again up at the ceiling for an instant, as if trying to shut down the music with his cold stare.

I practically shouted at him. "Boyd, why don't you put that gun away? Let's talk . . ."

And then I saw Eddie Greene racing down the hallway, his scooter going full speed.

Bruton saw or sensed the approach. But too late. Eddie Greene slammed the scooter into the back of Bruton's legs and sent him sprawling. His arms went up in the air and the pistol discharged. Loud. My ears rang. The bullet went into the ceiling above my head.

Bruton was stretched out on the floor on his stomach, his arms spread out in front him. Jerking my arm away from Elly, I took three long steps, and stomped hard on Bruton's wrist that held the gun. I stomped again. He gave a loud, guttural curse of anger and pain, words jumbled together, the sound coming from the back of his throat. He tried to squirm away, but he released the gun and I kicked at it, sending it scooting only a few inches from his outstretched fingers. I slammed my foot back on his wrist. He groaned again. I dropped to my knees, pounding them into his back. I rode high on his back like I was atop a walrus. Elly rushed closer and used her foot to push the gun a couple of feet away. Bruton flailed his left arm out, trying to reach back to dislodge me. I grabbed his arm and twisted hard.

Eddie Greene's eyes were wide and focused. He kept the scooter up against Bruton's legs.

From around the corner, at a full run, here came Balls and Deputy Odell Wright.

Even with me on top of him, Bruton rolled to one side in an effort to scramble up, to get up on his knees. I got pitched partly off of Bruton but before he could get up, Balls smashed his own knee onto the center of Bruton's back and twisted Bruton's arms, clamping on handcuffs in one swift movement. I'd never seen Balls move so fast.

The volume of the music went down. My ears still rang from the shot Bruton sent into the ceiling.

Balls and Wright got Bruton to his feet, his hands cuffed behind him. From up the hall from the direction of the candy section, a woman came scurrying down, holding tightly to the hand of a small young girl. As they hurried past us, an anxious look on the woman's face, the little girl said, "Mama, they're arresting Santa Claus."

I said, "He's not the real Santa Claus. He's not the real one."

Elly held on to my arm again, and touched her head briefly against my shoulder. I looked down at her. "You okay?" I said.

She managed to nod.

Eddie Greene looked up at the ceiling. "Richard can fix that," he said.

Elly stepped forward and took Eddie Greene's hand. "You saved us," she said. She didn't let go of his hand.

The usual twinkle came back into Eddie Greene's eyes. "Running the Christmas Shop has always been . . . been challenging," he said. He smiled. There was a look of real pride on his face. He knew he had saved the day.

Balls and Wright got set to lead Bruton away. Bruton didn't resist. He kept his head down and somehow he appeared deflated, as if he knew it was all over. Balls glanced

back at me, Elly, and Mr. Greene and for just an instant there
was the slightest trace of a smile on his face. Maybe it was
satisfaction or gratitude. Or relief that it was all over. I don't
know.

Epilogue

Rick Schweikert will prosecute the case against Boyd Bruton. Bruton is charged with premeditated murder of the two hit men, drug trafficking and conspiracy to commit murder with the Applewaite brothers and Ball's CI Leroy. A charge to be added, according to Schweikert, is the killing of Willie Boy Applewaite. I think Schweikert will do a good job. He is certainly looking forward to it with pride. He walks around town with more of a swagger than usual, and his shirts are even more stiffly starched nowadays.

Ballistics tests of the gun Bruton had in the Christmas Shop established that it was the weapon used to slay the two hit men found in the BMW at The Marketplace at Southern Shores. While not totally conclusive, tests show that it was the weapon used also to blast two holes in Willie Boy's chest. That certainly helps Schweikert's case.

The lab report that Balls was waiting for from the SBI lab technicians had to do with the partial palm print found on the trunk of the BMW. On a hunch, Balls had saved the most current petition that Linda Shackleford had brought him, and sent it to the lab. There were many fingerprints on the page, but one was of significant value: Next to his bold large signature was that of Boyd Bruton. Bruton's print matched the partial found on the trunk of the BMW.

Thank goodness the lab called back to Balls with the

results just before he headed to the sheriff's office to talk with Ricker. And Ricker? He got the hell back to Pennsylvania and I doubt if he ever wants to come this way again. Bruton has hired for his defense an excellent high-powered lawyer from Raleigh named F. Bailey Porterman. I know Porterman is good, but I don't think he'll be able to do more than perhaps keep Bruton off death row. At least I know that Bruton's days of playing Santa Claus are over—unless he revives the role in prison.

The petition against Sheriff Albright withered and died quickly. That doesn't mean that Patsy Davies will be energetically pushing some other cause shortly. I'm sure of that.

Things are more peaceful here now on the Outer Banks, and we're all looking forward to spring.

Oh, yes, Richard patched that bullet hole in the ceiling of the Christmas Shop. And Elly finished the season working there on weekends.

Mr. Greene is basking in the glory of his act of heroism. So now he has another story to tell concerning his interesting life.

And Balls? He's involved in another case. This one down beyond Stumpy Point. A rather reclusive woman who had befriended and fed some of the black bears for years was found near her home on an old logging road. It appeared she was mauled by a bear, but Balls isn't sure that's what happened.

Balls and Lorraine are talking about how much fun it would be to go back to Paris in the spring. I've mentioned this to Elly. Her eyes light up. As far as the history club she and Gregory Loudermilk discussed, it may, indeed, get started. And me? I'm no longer jealous of Mr. Perfect. But I'll keep my eyes on him just the same.

And at editor Rose Mantelli's urging, I've started another book. This one based on the case just ended. It's practically writing itself. Rose is convinced it'll get picked up for another TV movie like an earlier one did. Nice big chunk of change is always welcome.

Tonight Elly and I are going out to eat, probably at Kelly's, and I've promised I'm going to cook for her again soon, a beef dish that is in the Julia Child book.

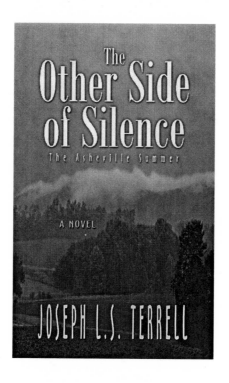

The Other Side Of Silence

The Asheville Summer

ISBN 978-1-933523-10-1

That summer in the mountains near Asheville, North Carolina, between the end of the Great Depression and the onset of World War II promised to be an enchanted one for ten-year-old Jonathan Clayton and his family. But almost from the beginning, Jonathan sensed that something sinister lived across the meadow at the base of Clown Mountain in the Dennihan's pigpen of a house. Before the summer ended, violence erupted in that house and Jonathan, his brother, sister, and cousins have to race ahead of a crazed, hatchet-wielding mountain man in a frantic flight to save their lives and stop their pursuer—by any means they can.

CPSIA information can be obtained
at www.ICGtesting.com
Printed in the USA
FFOW05n0823210515

9 781622 680795